CW01177770

MIKE GARRETT

DENNIS H. WILLIAMS

Copyright © 2024 by Dennis H. Williams

All rights reserved. No part of this publication may be reproduced, stored in a retrieval system or transmitted, in any form, or by any means, electronic, mechanical, recorded, photocopied, or otherwise, without the prior written permission of both the copyright owner and the publisher, except by a reviewer who may quote brief passages in a review.

The scanning, uploading, and distribution of this book via the Internet or via any other means without the permission of the publisher is illegal and punishable by law. Please purchase only authorized electronic editions and do not participate in or encourage piracy of copywritten material.

This is a work of fiction. Names, characters, places and incidents either are a product of the author's imagination or are used fictitiously, and any resemblance to actual persons, living or dead, business establishments, events, or locales is purely coincidental.

This book may contain views, premises, depictions, and statements by the author that are not necessarily shared or endorsed by Outlaws Publishing.

For information contact: info@outlawspublishing.com
Editor Michael Clement
Cover design by Outlaws Publishing.
Published by Outlaws Publishing.
November 2024
10 9 8 7 6 5 4 3 2 1

Dedicated to Mike Garrison

HIGH CALL

My, How Times Have Changed

In 1978 Larry Goss and Mike Garrison (pictured) won the Bob Feist Invitational Team Roping Classic by roping six steers in 81.42 seconds on a 35-foot score in Chowchilla, Calif. The fast time on one steer that year was 9.23 seconds, set by Jim Peterson and John Rodriguez. Goss and Garrison's average win is the second-slowest in the history of the event, while Peterson and Rodriguez's single-steer mark is the slowest in that category.

Part I: Homecoming

Chapter 1

For three days, the rain had fallen off and on, one wave of tropical moisture after another rolling through the southern Arizona deserts. It hadn't rained like this in four long years, a drought that had scorched the ranges, dried up waterholes and tanks, and left wells bone dry. Cattle had been sold off, herds thinned to preserve what little vegetation remained for the meager few left behind. Now, this soft, steady rain was saving the land and the livelihoods of countless ranchers.

Clifford Boss and his wife, Vera, sat on the porch of their modest, weather-worn ranch house, watching rainwater cascade from the porch roof in a shimmering curtain. Clifford held a water glass half-filled with whiskey, the amber liquid catching the muted light, while Vera cradled a skein of yarn in her lap, her fingers deftly working as she crocheted. They both seemed to absorb the moisture like parched earth, taking in the rejuvenation the rain brought.

The yard between the house and the corrals, once a dusty expanse of powdered dirt, had turned into a sea of mud. Thin rivulets of water snaked their way down toward the creek that bordered the ranch headquarters. The wash, dry for so long, now brimmed with rushing water, carrying away the debris and remnants of four years of relentless heat and hardship. Clifford took off his hat, revealing slightly graying hair matted by the damp, and allowed the cool moisture to seep into his scalp. Vera glanced over at him, a gentle smile touching her lips as strands of her own gray-shot hair fell around her shoulders.

For thirty years, they had weathered life together—through prosperity and hardship, joy and crushing disappointment. They had raised two sons to manhood under this roof. This little ranch, with its peeling paint and worn-out boards, had been their haven and their anchor. Yet, the relentless drought had forced them to sell off so many cattle that now only a handful remained, just enough to scrape by. But at least the ranch was paid off, and the cattle they did have were theirs, free and clear. It was a foundation, a chance to start over.

Their oldest son had joined the Army right after high school and had fallen in Afghanistan. He lay in Arlington Cemetery, far from the Arizona land he once called home. On the bedroom dresser sat his photograph, flanked by his Medal of Honor and a carefully folded tri-cornered flag. His loss had hollowed out a part of Clifford, leaving him bitter and withdrawn. Vera had tried, in her gentle and persistent way, to pull him back from that dark place, but she always seemed to run up against an invisible wall, unyielding and cold.

Their youngest, Donnie, had gone off to community college on a rodeo scholarship. He hadn't come back home, caught up in the whirlwind of the rodeo circuit, traveling from one small town to the next with his best friend. Through it all, Clifford and Vera had kept the ranch alive, with Vera working tirelessly beside her husband. She rode out nearly every day, just as Clifford did. She cooked, cleaned, mended fences, and rode the trails without complaint, hoping that their shared labor might bring Clifford back to her in spirit as well as body.

The rain had eased now, turning into a light, misting drizzle. Clifford took another sip of his whiskey, savoring the warmth it spread through him, when the sharp trill of the phone rang from inside the house. He rose with a groan, his joints stiff from years of hard work, and disappeared into the dim interior.

Moments later, he returned, his expression dark and furrowed. "Better get Donnie's room ready," he said, his voice rough with unspoken worry. "Mike's bringing him home. He'll be laid up for a while. He's hurt pretty bad, I guess."

Vera's hands stilled on the yarn as she looked up, eyes wide with concern. "What happened?"

Clifford's jaw tightened, and for a moment, the rain was the only sound between them, pattering softly on the roof and washing away the dust of their long drought.

The next morning, Clifford could hear a truck turn off the main road onto the half-mile driveway to the ranch. As it grew closer, he could see a white Ford truck pulling a blue four-horse trailer. It slid sideways in places on the muddy road, but with tires spinning, it pushed on into the yard and rolled to a stop at the gate by the house. From the driver's side emerged a short, stocky, sandy-haired young man—Mike Garrett. He walked around to the passenger side, where Clifford and Vera were waiting.

Shaking Clifford's hand, he said, "Good morning." Then he opened the passenger door, revealing Donnie. He still wore a hospital smock hanging from his neck, but his Wranglers and roper boots were on. His eyes were glazed over, his left eye black, and four stitches marked his brow. Mike reached in and unbuckled the seat belt, speaking softly, "We're home, Donnie."

Donnie nodded and tried to move, but a grimace of pain crossed his face. Turning to Clifford and Vera, Mike said, "He's got a concussion. But that's not the worst of it. Under his right rib cage, there's an eight-inch wound they sewed shut. Let's get him to bed, and I'll explain everything."

Clifford and Mike lifted Donnie out of the truck, holding him on either side as they carefully walked him to the house and into his bedroom. They sat him on the edge of the bed, gently pulling off his boots and jeans. When they laid him down, Vera caught sight of the angry red line of stitches across his abdomen. She sucked in a breath, her hand flying to her mouth.

Donnie's body relaxed as he closed his eyes, slipping into a deep sleep. Back in the kitchen, Vera poured everyone a cup of hot coffee. Outside, the rain had picked up again, a slow, steady drizzle. Mike took a sip of his coffee, then looked up.

"It was a bad wreck," he began. "His bulldogging horse dropped its feet in front of the steer, and they hoolihaned. The steer ran a horn into him. We don't know how the concussion happened. He's on serious painkillers—that's why he's out of it. The doctors had to remove four inches of damaged intestine. They're worried about infection. There's a bag of medicine in the truck—antibiotics and painkillers. Doc said no strenuous activity for six months. I've got his horses in the trailer; he said to turn them out until he's well."

Mike took another sip. "I tried to talk him out of entering the bulldogging. The stock there was rough, but the all-around paid an extra thousand. He'd already won second in the calf roping and was set to take third in team roping. But he said he needed to send you some cash because of the drought. He's been worried about you."

"We've been worried about him!" Clifford snorted. "We haven't heard a word in over a year. If it wasn't for the rodeo sports paper, we wouldn't even know where he was or what he was doing."

Chapter 2

The Gadsden Hotel in Douglas, Arizona, stood as a southern Arizona landmark, positioned almost at the heart of town with one of the best dining rooms around. That morning, a tall, dark-skinned man sat at a table enjoying his breakfast of huevos rancheros smothered in chili sauce. Ramundo Cortez-Coronado, dressed like any Sonoran rancher in denim pants, boots, and a floral print shirt, was no simple ranchero. His interests spanned various businesses along the border, most of them of dubious legality. Today, he operated as a palmero—a contractor harvesting bear grass used by Mexican laborers in Agua Prieta to manufacture place mats, door mats, and trinkets in a sweatshop he owned.

Finishing his meal, Ramundo left a five-dollar tip and settled the tab with a wad of greenbacks thick enough to choke one of his pack burros. Flashing a gold-toothed smile at the young waitress, he strode out the door and climbed into his Chevy four-by-four. His destination lay east, toward a ranch known for its hills abundant with bear grass. The couple running the place had been struggling financially, and he had once expected to own it, had the rains not come. Though they had been spared for now, Ramundo knew their livestock numbers were meager and their finances tight—perfect conditions for him to leverage when the time came.

Back at the ranch, Cliff, Vera, and Donnie were seated on the front porch, enjoying the fresh, rain-cooled air when a pale blue Ford pickup pulled into the yard. The engine idled before stopping, and out stepped a tall, auburn-haired woman with an hourglass figure. Her Wranglers fit snugly, as did the T-shirt emblazoned with a vintage 1920s cowgirl riding a bucking bronco.

Donnie rose slowly, a wide smile spreading across his face. Cliff and Vera followed suit, eyes full of anticipation. The woman approached the porch with determined strides, and Donnie stepped forward to meet her, embracing her carefully.

"Mom, Dad, this is Jordon, my fiancée," Donnie announced.

Before Cliff could extend his hand or offer a greeting, Vera pushed past him, wrapping Jordon in a warm hug. "Welcome to the family!" she said, her voice full of affection.

Cliff smiled, bowing slightly at the waist. "It's a pleasure to meet you. Make yourself at home."

At first, Jordon's eyes reflected a hint of hesitation, but the genuine welcome brightened her face. She beamed at Donnie. "How are you feeling, honey?"

Donnie's grin widened. "Better than I should, now that you're here." When she moved to hug him, he pulled back with a chuckle. "Nope, not yet. I'll do the hugging."

He slipped an arm around her waist and turned to his parents.

"Jordon is a registered nurse. She quit her job at the Deming hospital to be with me. I think I'll heal a lot faster with her here."

"Well, I don't see how you can keep from it!" Cliff laughed, the warmth in his eyes mirrored by the soft, early morning light spilling across the porch.

Chapter 3

The white Chevy 4x4 rolled into the ranch yard, the engine purring as it slowed to a stop. Dust billowed in the dry air, swirling in little clouds around the tires before settling again. Cliff was coming from the corrals, wiping his hands on his jeans as he approached the truck, his boots crunching on the gravel. Donnie was sitting on the porch, the sun's heat still lingering on the wood slats beneath him. In the kitchen, Vera and Jordon were talking quietly, the sounds of dishes clinking and a door creaking open.

A tall, dark man climbed out of the Chevy, his movements precise, almost rehearsed. Cliff took in the man's sharp appearance—cowboy boots polished to a high gloss, a slim-brimmed straw hat perched atop his head, casting a shadow over his sharp features. The man sidestepped a puddle, making a concerted effort not to dirty his boots, his expression a practiced blend of professionalism and confidence.

Cliff's eyes flicked to Donnie, who had a sour look on his face, eyes narrowing at the sight of the stranger. It was a look Cliff knew well—one that said trouble might be coming, or at the very least, that the man wasn't to be trusted.

The stranger approached, his movements smooth, his smile just a little too controlled. "Señor, I'm here to ask about your bear grass harvest," he said, his voice carrying a thick accent, yet his words clear. "My name is Ramundo. My business is Palmero."

He extended his hand, and Cliff shook it, the firm grip solid but not overwhelming. As their hands met, Ramundo's fingers were warm, his palm dry, and Cliff could almost feel the practiced ease in the man's demeanor, like this was something he had done a thousand times before.

"Well, I hadn't thought much about the bear grass," Cliff said, his voice carrying a slight note of curiosity. "Didn't know it had any value. What sort of deal you got in mind?"

Ramundo's eyes gleamed, and his smile didn't falter. "I will bring six men, four burros, and all the equipment and supplies," he said smoothly, every word coming with a sense of finality. "They will cut the bear grass, bundle it, and I will come every other day to haul it back to Mexico. When I come, I will bring the supplies. Every time I haul a load, I will pay you a hundred dollars. When the work is done, the camp will be clean, your cattle will not be bothered. This, I promise."

Cliff mulled it over, his brow furrowing slightly. It seemed almost too good to be true. Ramundo had it all laid out, no hesitations, no ambiguities. Just a clean deal.

He glanced at Donnie, who still looked unsettled, his lips pressed into a tight line. Donnie was usually a man of few words, but when something didn't sit right with him, it was clear as day.

"Sounds alright, but I want a day or so to talk it over with my wife and son," Cliff said, his tone calm but thoughtful. "I can call you when we decide."

Ramundo didn't blink. Instead, he reached into his wallet with fluid precision, pulling out a business card and handing it to Cliff. As he opened his wallet, Cliff caught sight of the thick wad of greenbacks stuffed inside. It was subtle, but not by much. Ramundo made sure Cliff noticed.

"Call me anytime during the day," Ramundo said, his voice smooth, with just a hint of finality. "If I'm not there, my secretary will tell me you called, and I'll return the call. Thank you, Señor, for your time."

Without another word, he turned and climbed back into the Chevy, the engine growling to life. As the truck began to pull away, Jordon and Vera stepped out onto the porch. Vera's movements were slow, measured, as though she had all the time in the world, while Jordon, her eyes scanning the truck, had a quick, almost wary look about her.

But it was Jordon who caught Ramundo's attention. His head snapped around, his eyes locking onto her for a brief, split second, before he turned his focus back to the road. The brief encounter left a strange tension in the air, and Cliff couldn't help but notice the way Ramundo's eyes lingered on Jordon before he accelerated out of the yard, tires kicking up dust in his wake.

Cliff walked back up to the porch, the card still in his hand. He handed it to Donnie, who took it but didn't look at it right away. Instead, he rubbed his hand through his hair, the motion jerking him in a way that made him wince, and blood trickled from the corner of the cut above his eye, tracing down his skin in a thin, crimson line.

"What do you think?" Cliff asked, trying to read his son's expression.

Donnie's brow furrowed, his gaze flitting from the card to the dust cloud now hanging in the air where the Chevy had been. "We sure could use the cash," he muttered, his voice low. "We wouldn't have to dip into our cattle for the rest of the winter." He paused, the card still in his hand, his fingers tightening around it as if trying to crush the decision into something more definite. "But that guy... he looks too slick. Like he's putting on a front." He ran his hand through his hair again, smearing the blood across his temple. "But yeah, the cash flow would come in handy."

Vera took the card from Donnie, her fingers soft but steady as she examined it for a moment before passing it to Jordon. "It would keep the grocery bill in check. Donnie eats like a horse!" she added with a chuckle.

Jordon smiled at Vera's joke, but then the smile faded, and she gave the card a thoughtful glance. "I'm the outsider here," she said, her voice light but honest. "I appreciate you including me in, but this is your ranch. I'm just a nurse for a beat-up cowboy."

Everyone laughed, the tension lifting for the moment. There were more smiles now than frowns, and the warm sunlight, the smell of fresh bread from the kitchen, and the distant hum of the wind through the trees all combined into a feeling of peace that had been sorely missing.

Vera had set up a rollaway bed in Donnie's room for Jordon. It was an arrangement they had all fallen into without much fuss. Jordon had taken over the nursing duties, allowing Vera to cook for the four of them. The routine had become comfortable—slowly but surely, Donnie was starting to get up and move around again, his pace still slow but steady, his body healing with each passing day.

Jordon made sure he kept up with his antibiotics, but she kept a sharp eye on him, making sure he didn't take too many pain pills, watching for signs of dependence. He was tough, she knew, but that didn't mean he didn't need help. She knew when to push and when to hold back, when to give him space, and when to make him rest. Each day, Donnie needed fewer pills, and his movements grew less stiff.

Jordon had checked the local hospital in Douglas before coming to the ranch. It came highly recommended, and she planned on taking Donnie there for a check-up the next day. Vera was going to come along to do some shopping—there was always something to pick up in town.

It felt good to be settling into this rhythm. Even in the quiet moments, the house felt like it was healing. There were no more strained silences between them, no more hard stares. Just a quiet, almost unspoken agreement that, for now, they were family.

The sun was barely breaking over the horizon when Raemundo made his call. His two-and-a-half-ton International bobtail truck, already loaded two-thirds of the way, stood ready for the final preparations. His burros were packed, and his six helpers awaited their signal. The camp supplies—tools, gear, and everything needed for the harvest—were already secured in the back, snug under the false floor. All that remained was to load the burros, pick up the men, and start the journey.

As he maneuvered the truck toward the border crossing, Raemundo's mind raced with quiet excitement. His heart beat with a familiar rhythm—the thrill of a routine well-executed. The border guards knew him well by now. They saw him often enough that he'd become almost a fixture, the picture of a hard-working rancher from Sonora. There was never a reason to doubt him.

He handed over the work visas for his men and the health papers for the burros, watching the guards as they shuffled through the documents. Meanwhile, a guard with a long pole-mounted mirror slowly circled the truck, peering under it for anything that seemed out of place. It was a process they'd done a hundred times before, but Raemundo had a quiet confidence, knowing the truck would clear without issue.

The guard checked between the gaps in the side boards, his boots scraping the dirt as he circled the truck. The moment stretched on, but not for Raemundo. His grin tugged at the corner of his lips. He knew the procedure by heart, and he knew the truck well. Beneath the heavy layers of equipment, the sturdy wood, and the thick canvas tarps, a false floor hid the real cargo. At a mere 14 inches deep, it was enough to conceal all manner of contraband—human cargo, merchandise, and other goods that slipped by unnoticed. The guards never looked hard enough. And this time, it wasn't just bundles of bear grass that would be crossing the border.

Minutes passed, and finally, the truck was cleared. The guard waved them on, and Raemundo shifted gears, pulling the truck forward onto the eastbound road. The familiar, dusty landscape of Douglas quickly faded behind him as the open road beckoned. He felt a small surge of satisfaction—another easy pass. The grin stretched wider on his face, the road ahead empty and waiting.

What no one knew—what no one had yet figured out—was that this truck wasn't just hauling bear grass. Beneath the floorboards, stretched out like silent passengers, were four Mexican nationals. They lay hidden, cramped and cold in their makeshift space. They'd paid handsomely for the one-way ride—enough money to make up for the loss of three months of harvest. They were headed to Phoenix, but the road there was long, and the price of a safe passage was steep. But once they'd left Raemundo's camp, they would be on their own. He'd never look back.

Raemundo's eyes narrowed as he turned up the dusty road toward the ranch. He bounced over the uneven terrain, the truck's suspension groaning in protest. As he reached the yard, he spotted Cliff waiting for him, the rancher's sturdy frame casting a shadow on the morning light. Raemundo waved, giving a nod of acknowledgment, before Cliff approached to give him directions to the best campsite.

Minutes later, Raemundo was unloading the truck, his boots crunching in the dirt as he worked with his crew. They set up the camp efficiently, pulling out tents, stakes, and gear. When the work was done, he turned back to the truck. He lifted three wooden boards from the floor with a practiced hand, and there, hidden away in the cramped space, were the four men. Their eyes blinked at the sudden light, disoriented and stiff from the long ride.

Raemundo handed them each a bundle—a moral, a few tortillas, and a jug of water. His eyes met theirs, unreadable as ever. "You know the way," he said in a low voice. "Head north from here, find a ride to Phoenix. I'll be gone before you even get there."

The men didn't respond, only nodded, their eyes shifting nervously. They had no choice now but to walk the rest of the way, but at least they were alive. That, in Raemundo's world, was worth the price they paid.

Once the men were gone, Raemundo turned back to the campfire, his face shadowed by the flickering flames. He would wait for his crew to finish gathering the bear grass. They had a few days of hard work ahead, and Raemundo would oversee it all, just like he always did. But in the back of his mind, his plans were already forming. This load was only the beginning. His next shipment would be waiting for him, just around the bend.

And when it came to his contraband—well, as long as it didn't involve drugs, Raemundo could keep his operation running smoothly, undetected, and profitable. He wasn't foolish enough to get involved in cartel dealings. That was a dead end, a line that shouldn't be crossed. But the rest of the business? The deals he'd made with the other side of the border were his to handle, and he was good at it. No one had ever caught him, and no one ever would.

The camp settled into a rhythm—burros tied to posts, men working with machetes to cut the grass and bundle it for transport. Raemundo watched them, his mind already turning over the next move. It wasn't just about the bear grass anymore. It was about what he could bring back, and what he could get away with.

The sun sank low in the sky, casting long shadows over the barren land. And Raemundo, ever the calculating operator, was already planning his next trip across the border.

Chapter 4

Donnie stood on the porch of the house, leaning slightly against the post that supported the roof. His back ached, but the fresh air felt good against his skin. He'd just returned from his check-up with the Mexican doctor in Douglas. The visit had gone well, and everything was healing as it should. Even the doctor had given the go-ahead for Jordon to remove the stitches over his eye, something Donnie wasn't quite ready to look at just yet. His face still felt tender, but at least it wasn't the throbbing pain it had been when he first got hurt.

Vera had filled the back of the truck with food staples—flour, sugar, coffee, and canned goods. Donnie couldn't help but feel a little uneasy, though. He worried she might've stretched the bank account too thin this time. It wasn't that he didn't appreciate everything they were doing for him, but the weight of it all started to press down on him. Out there in the yard, Cliff was making a deal with a Palmaro who would bring in a steady cash flow for a while. That was something. Donnie glanced at his father, and a sense of relief washed over him. Cliff and Vera still wouldn't let him pay for anything around here, and he couldn't deny how much it humbled him. Jordon had pitched in too, doing double duty as both nurse and housekeeper, helping around the barn, and even tending to the corrals when she could.

The doctor had been clear: Donnie wasn't to strain himself, not yet. He had to be careful, or he could tear internal stitches along with the external ones. Still, he was getting stronger. Though still sore, he could walk around and help out with little tasks here and there. But there was something else, a gnawing feeling he couldn't shake. For reasons he couldn't explain, he didn't trust Raemundo, the Palmaro. It was a gut instinct—one that dug at him whenever he thought about the man.

The next day, Cliff suggested that he, Donnie, and Jordon take a slow ride around the ranch in the truck. It wasn't a long drive, but Cliff thought it would do Donnie some good to get out, to see a little more of the ranch. And, maybe, just maybe, he hoped Donnie might think about staying on when he was fully healed.

When they climbed into the truck the following morning, Donnie noticed something unusual. A picture of his brother was clipped to the visor above Cliff's head. He nudged Jordon with his elbow and nodded toward the picture. Jordon met his gaze briefly before averting her eyes, a quiet tension filling the cab. Cliff, noticing the moment, spoke up. "With you gone, he keeps me company sometimes." He flipped the visor up, his voice soft, but there was an edge of longing there.

For three hours, they bumped along the ranch roads. The air smelled of dry earth and the faint scent of sagebrush. Occasionally, they passed a cow and her calf grazing in the distance. The rustle of leaves and the scurrying of javelina broke the silence around them. But mostly, the ride was quiet, with the sound of the truck's tires crunching over gravel and dirt beneath them. Donnie watched the landscape pass by, but his thoughts were elsewhere, swirling around that nagging feeling about Raemundo.

Soon, they came into view of the Palmaro camp. From a distance, they could hear the high-pitched whine of a two-cycle motor and the rhythmic hum of something cutting through the thick brush. The red International bobtail sat parked, surrounded by scattered camp gear. Donnie noticed the growing pile of bear grass bundles stacked neatly near the truck. Cliff slowed the truck to a stop, watching the workers from the side of the road. The men were busy with motorized weed eaters, each one fitted with a saw blade, cutting through the tough, fibrous bear grass. The sound of the blade slicing through the plant rang out sharply, the noise grating on Donnie's nerves.

One of the men was leading a pair of burros, each one heavily laden with bundles of bear grass. Behind him, another man was raking the fronds into a neat pile, rolling them into tight bundles, and tying them together with twine. Two other burros stood off to the side, waiting for Raemundo to load them up. When they were packed, the burros barely showed above the piles of bundles—just their heads and tails visible.

Cliff started the truck again, but Donnie's attention remained fixed on the camp. The uneasy feeling still hadn't left him. As they pulled away, Cliff glanced over at him. "You alright?" he asked. "Am I driving too rough?"

Donnie shook his head, trying to push the discomfort aside. "No, I'm good. You're fine. Just get a pain sometimes... nothing to worry about." He tried to brush it off, but his mind was elsewhere. Raemundo was still nagging at him.

That evening, as they sat down for supper, Donnie cleared his throat. "We need to have a pow-wow tonight, Dad," he said. "Unless you've got other plans?"

Cliff looked up from his plate, his brow furrowed for a moment before he grinned. "After supper, okay? If it's something serious, I don't want to spoil the meal." He laughed, but Donnie could tell his dad wasn't entirely at ease with the idea.

"It's nothing like that," Donnie replied, grinning back. "But I think we need to make a plan. You, Mom, Jordon, and me. We all need to talk." His gaze shifted to Jordon, a light smile playing at the corner of his lips.

Jordon met his eyes and gave him a small nod, but Donnie could tell she was just as thoughtful, her expression more reserved. There was something about this place, this ranch, that seemed to draw out more than just the people who lived here—it was as if the land itself held secrets, and Donnie wasn't sure he was ready to face them all just yet.

When Donnie and Jordon stepped out of the bank in downtown Douglas, the first thing they saw was the red International bobtail rolling by, piled high with bundles of bear grass. The truck rumbled past, its engine grumbling low against the dry morning air, as Raemundo sat behind the wheel, staring straight ahead on his way to the border crossing.

"I can't help it," Donnie muttered, his eyes narrowing slightly as the truck disappeared down the street. "I don't like that guy. Can't tell you why—I've never even met him—but something just don't ring true."

Jordon shot him a sidelong glance, her expression unreadable but intrigued. "You think so? Maybe he's just got that border-town aura. Could be nothing."

Donnie shook his head, still feeling the uneasy stir inside him. As they walked toward his truck, the distant scent of desert dust mixed with the faint tang of diesel from the truck still lingering in the air, the weight of yesterday's conversation pressed on his mind.

He remembered sitting down with Jordon, Vera, and Cliff the night before, the warm amber glow from the fireplace casting long shadows over the living room. Vera had poured them each a stiff drink as Donnie laid out his proposal, his voice steady, but the sense of uncertainty in the air was palpable.

"I want us to buy a mobile home," Donnie had said, his hands nervously clasped in his lap. "Set it up at the ranch when Jordon and I get married. And we'll buy some cows—enough to match what you and Vera have left. You two will own the ranch, but Jordon and I—well, we'll be partners in the grass."

Vera's face had brightened at the idea, her eyes sparkling with excitement, but Donnie could feel Cliff's gaze weighing heavily on him, like he was trying to see through Donnie, through his plans, trying to figure out if he was truly serious. The room felt heavy with the weight of family tradition, and Donnie could see the old man wrestling with the decision, each word more deliberate than the last.

"The last part of it," Donnie continued, his voice a little firmer now, "is that Jordon and I will pay a share of the operating costs, at least until we sell a calf crop. And that starts now."

Cliff had stared down at his glass for a long moment, his fingers rubbing along the edge of it as his eyes glazed over. Finally, he'd looked up, his expression unreadable. He cleared his throat, his voice thick with emotion.

"Son, this ranch is your home for as long as you want it to be," he said quietly, his voice carrying a weight of years and memories. "Your mom and I raised you here. I always hoped one of you boys would come back. I guess it's hard for your mom and me to break that habit of feeding, clothing, and educating you. I don't know how much money you've got, and honestly, I don't need to know. I just want you to have a fair shot at making a go of it. If it means your mom and I go without for a bit, then that's part of the deal."

Donnie felt a lump form in his throat, the sincerity in Cliff's voice catching him off guard. Cliff's eyes were moist, but he held them steady, not wanting to show too much emotion.

"You're not going to be much help physically for a while," Cliff continued, his voice softer now, "but that's okay. I'm sure the time will come when I won't be either. So, if your mom and Jordon are in agreement, I'm in."

Cliff held up his glass, his eyes locking with Donnie's, and in that moment, Donnie knew that this was about more than just business—it was about family, loyalty, and trust.

No one spoke for a long moment. But in the silence, they all raised their glasses in unison, the clink of glass echoing in the warm, heavy air.

Later, at the bank, Donnie had Jordon's name added to his account. He transferred $2,000 into the ranch account, knowing it was a start—a solid foundation for what was to come. He and Jordon had also set up a line of credit, a safety net for the future. Over the past 18 months, Donnie had kept enough of his rodeo winnings to keep him in the game and deposited the rest. It had built up into a nice little nest egg, a cushion for the future.

In his shirt pocket, he carried a draft book. He couldn't work just yet, but his mind was always running, always planning. And Jordon—she was with him every step of the way, no complaints, no arguments. She was a steady presence by his side, as constant as the desert sun.

When Donnie asked her about the wedding, she just smiled, her voice light and easy. "I want my folks there, my sister, and your folks. That's enough. Maybe the preacher, huh?"

She laughed, and Donnie felt a warmth spread through him. "Well, I'll track down Mike and get him here. I need a best man, and Lord knows where he's at. I think I'll be able to stand up long enough for the ceremony, and maybe be okay with being bounced around later."

Donnie grinned, the uncertainty of the future melting away for a moment. They still had a long way to go, but this was the first step. Together, they could make it.

It was still early, so they drove over to Sierra Vista, to a lot that sold mobile homes. Donnie stayed in the office while Jordon and the salesman toured the houses. The faint smell of fresh paint and wood lingered in the office, mingling with the dry scent of the desert outside.

When Jordon came back, she had a pamphlet in her hand, a floor plan of a small, simple two-bedroom house. She handed it to Donnie, her smile bright and sure.

"You sure?" he asked, studying the design with a raised brow.

Jordon smiled and nodded. "Home sweet home."

At the ranch that morning, Raemundo had stopped, counted out $100 in twenty-dollar bills, and made sure the first load of bear grass was shipped out. He had promised Cliff he'd be back in two days.

Cliff handed the money to Vera, his rough hands lingering on hers for a moment. "Better stash that for the next bill of groceries," he said, his voice low and practical.

Cliff turned and walked out the door, heading toward the barn. He saddled a horse, humming a tune as he set out to check the cows. The desert air was still cool from the night, but the warmth of the sun would be rising soon.

Chapter 5

A few weeks later, Donnie approached Cliff at supper. "Will you drive me to Willcox tomorrow for the auction? They've got a good run of young cows coming through. I'd like to pick up a few. Jordon is still getting her house done up."

"Okay, sounds like a good day to pick up some ranch supplies too," Cliff replied with a smile. He had been waiting for Donnie to start gathering a herd, but between the mobile home delivery and setup, they hadn't had time for much else.

The next day at the auction barn, Cliff and Donnie walked the aisles, examining the bred cows and pairs. Donnie jotted down tag numbers of the groups he wanted to bid on. Cliff couldn't help but feel a swell of pride as Donnie made his picks. His son was sharp, calculating—the kind of man who would make a go of it. But Cliff knew it wouldn't come cheap. A couple of big-spending buyers were in the mix, their deep pockets well-known.

By the time the sale wrapped up that afternoon, Donnie had bought 40 pairs and 80 bred cows, all due to calve in the next 30 days. Two truckloads. Cliff was stunned. He hadn't realized Donnie had the financial resources to make a purchase like that. It was more than a gamble—it was a big, bold step.

When Donnie hobbled into the office to pay, he approached the blonde girl behind the desk. She looked up, her eyes widening. "You're Donnie Boss!" she exclaimed. He nodded with a grin.

"I need to pay for these cattle," Donnie said, pulling his draft book from his shirt pocket.

"We see you at all the rodeos. My friends and I follow you. You'll be a world champion one day!" the girl blurted out, her voice a mix of awe and excitement.

Donnie raised a hand. "Please, just let me pay for these cattle."

The girl blinked, then slid an invoice across the counter. Donnie began to fill it out.

"I'll want these cattle branded before delivery," he said, passing the draft and a list of vaccines back to her. "And I'd like them trucked to the ranch as well."

"We can do that," the girl replied. "The vaccines and processing will cost two dollars a head. I can't quote the trucking, but we'll get it arranged. You can pay them direct."

"Sounds good. Delivery by Monday—does that work?"

She nodded, her pen pausing mid-sentence before looking up at him. "This draft has Jordon Boss listed too. Is she…?"

"Yes," Donnie said with a smile, "she'll be my wife. And yes, she's the barrel racer and breakaway roper." He started to turn to leave. "I'll go grab the irons from the truck. When they bring the cattle Monday, make sure the irons are on the truck too, okay?"

"I'll go get the irons. You sit for a bit," Cliff said, gripping Donnie's arm gently and nodding toward his side. A red stain was showing through his shirt.

Donnie hesitated but then eased into a leather chair in the lobby. "Okay, I'll wait here."

At the Bear Grass warehouse in Agua Prieta, Raemundo was loading supplies for the ranch. His operation was running smoothly—every load he took back paid the bills and left the Bear Grass business in the clear. Sometimes, he hauled liquor or prescription drugs in the false floor. Other times, it was people. They paid the best, with cash up front. There hadn't been a question from the authorities, so far.

Today, he wasn't sure what he would take, but before he could decide, he sensed a presence behind him. Turning, he saw a young Mexican man—heavyset, tattoos snaking across his neck. His eyes, cold and calculating, gave Raemundo the shivers, like a rattlesnake ready to strike.

"I've got a load for you to take across the line. It pays well," the man said flatly.

Raemundo felt a prickle of unease. "I'm not doing business with the cartel. I have my own operations to worry about."

The man's smile didn't reach his eyes. "We're not the cartel. These aren't drugs. It pays five thousand to drive them across."

He pulled a roll of fresh hundred-dollar bills from his pocket and began counting them. Raemundo's gaze flicked to the money.

"What am I hauling, and where do I take it?" Raemundo asked, trying to focus despite the tightness in his chest.

"You'll be met on the other side. They'll lead you to the unloading spot," the man answered, his voice devoid of warmth.

Raemundo didn't answer right away, but two other tattooed men appeared, carrying plastic-wrapped bundles. Some were long, others short, some small enough to fit in the palm of his hand. He pulled the floorboards back and let them load the truck.

"I don't haul drugs," Raemundo protested, his voice steady despite the tension coiling in his stomach.

"No drugs," the man assured him, slipping the cash into Raemundo's shirt pocket. "Just don't get caught. If you do, I'll want that back."

Once they left, Raemundo replaced the floorboards and backed the truck up to a manure pile. Sweating, he shoveled three inches of manure over the hidden floorboards, masking the cargo before heading for the border.

The weight of the situation pressed on him as his hands gripped the steering wheel, knuckles white, sweat trickling down his forehead like a river.

At the border, the usual guards checked his paperwork and scanned the truck, their scrutiny routine. They waved him through. A block from the gate, Raemundo pulled over and got out. A tattooed boy on a bike approached, nodding his head down the road.

Raemundo climbed back in the truck and followed the boy north out of Douglas.

Back at the checkpoint, the guard who had waved him through watched with suspicion. He made a call, his eyes narrowing as he noticed Raemundo's truck veering north instead of heading east.

Cliff came back into the sale barn office, his boots heavy against the concrete floor, the sharp tang of sawdust and livestock filling the air. He paused when he saw the secretary kneeling beside Donnie, holding a wet cloth against his side. The bright red stain seeping through his shirt sent a wave of panic through Cliff's chest.

"His bleeding's worse," the secretary said, her voice tight with concern. "I called the ambulance."

Donnie's face was ashen, and he was barely conscious, his breathing shallow. His lips, pale and cracked, parted as if to speak, but he seemed too weak to manage a word. Cliff felt his heart lurch in his chest.

"I was afraid this was too much, too soon," Cliff muttered, his hand gripping the doorframe as he watched Donnie's pale, almost lifeless form.

The ambulance arrived moments later, the sound of the sirens fading into the background as the EMTs worked quickly, their gloved hands swift and sure as they loaded Donnie onto a stretcher. Cliff could barely catch his breath as they transferred Donnie into the vehicle. The stench of antiseptic filled the air, mingling with the acrid scent of sweat that clung to Donnie's skin.

After a moment, one of the EMTs turned to Cliff, his voice calm but urgent. "He tore some stitches loose. We aren't supposed to, but we can staple them back in place."

Donnie, still semi-conscious, heard the words and managed to raise his head. A faint smile tugged at the corner of his lips, and he gave Cliff a wink, though it looked more like a grimace.

Cliff couldn't help but chuckle dryly. "What I don't know won't hurt me," he muttered, stepping away from the ambulance. He was grateful that Donnie's stubbornness hadn't completely broken him.

An hour later, they were headed back to the ranch. Donnie had slipped into a deep, much-needed nap, his face relaxed, his brow no longer furrowed in pain. The local anesthetic hadn't worn off yet, but the staples and fresh bandage seemed to have done their job. Donnie had admitted that he didn't know how he'd torn the stitches loose, but as far as he could remember, nothing he'd done had caused it.

The EMT had handed him a bag of medical supplies, instructing him to rest and follow up with a doctor. Donnie had nodded, agreeing to take it easy for once. They reminded him to avoid strenuous activity. He had agreed again, though his eyes said otherwise.

Above them, a silver helicopter hovered a thousand feet above the red International truck. Its rotors chopped through the thick desert air as a border patrol agent piloted it, an observer beside him scanning the landscape below. The truck, heading toward the ranch, turned off the pavement and onto a dirt road, the tires kicking up dust as it moved along. About a quarter mile in, it parked beside a Ford pickup with a shell camper, where a motorcyclist and two men from the truck began unloading packages, carefully stacking them in the bed of the Ford. The helicopter circled above, its presence unnoticed.

The red truck, now empty, returned to the asphalt and headed back toward Douglas, while the Ford drove toward I-10. The spotter in the helicopter reported the situation to the radio.

"Let the red truck go," came the order. "The Ford is the one we need to stop before it hits the interstate."

The helicopter followed the red truck all the way to its destination, the border patrol agent reporting the location. Meanwhile, the Ford continued toward the interstate, unaware of the deputies trailing behind it.

As they neared the entrance to I-10, a border patrol van and two county deputies' cars swarmed in behind them, lights flashing and sirens wailing. The driver, frantic, stomped on the gas, trying to outrun the pursuing vehicles. Up ahead, another deputy and a border patrol agent had already set up a roadblock. With nowhere to go, the Ford veered off the road at 90 miles per hour, crashing through a small mesquite tree and tearing through a barbed-wire fence. The truck whipped in an arc and slammed onto its side, metal groaning under the impact.

The passenger, a tattooed Mexican, scrambled out of the truck and began firing at the officers. The air rang with the sharp crack of gunfire as the deputies returned fire. It took only four shots to bring him down. The driver, still trapped in the wreckage, had already died in the crash.

The packages in the truck bed were plastic-wrapped and secured tightly, but it was immediately clear that they weren't what they appeared to be. As officers opened the truck doors, they found firearms stacked inside. A street map of Phoenix lay next to the driver's seat, with an address circled in bright red ink.

"This is one delivery not gonna make it to the gangs," said the senior deputy, a grim expression crossing his face as he surveyed the scene.

"We'll keep an eye on that Palmero truck," one of the officers suggested. "See where he's picking this stuff up. If he makes another delivery, we'll be ready."

All the way home, Donnie fidgeted in the passenger seat. It wasn't the pain that bothered him, but the tingling sensation as the local anesthetic wore off. His side felt strange, numb one moment and sensitive the next. He shifted, uncomfortable, his hand resting on the wound instinctively, though he knew better than to touch it too much.

Cliff glanced over at his son, shaking his head with a sigh. He could tell Donnie wasn't in real pain, but the tingling, the odd numbness, was wearing on him. "The sooner we get you back to Jordon, the sooner you'll feel better," he muttered, mostly to himself.

Jordon was waiting when they arrived at the ranch. She was at the door before they even got out of the truck, already reaching for Donnie's arm to steady him as he stepped down. The faint smell of antiseptic mixed with the dry desert air, and Jordon could see the pale, exhausted look on Donnie's face. He'd been through a lot.

She guided him to the living room, helping him sit down carefully. Cliff followed behind, grimacing at the thought of the EMT's makeshift stapling job. Jordon took a deep breath as she unbuttoned Donnie's shirt. The dried blood stuck to the fabric, and she grimaced as she carefully peeled it away.

"What's happening here, is the stitches rotting out?" she asked, her voice steady but tinged with concern. She could see that Donnie's side was swollen around the staples, a deep red hue surrounding the wound. "We probably need to restaple the whole deal," she muttered, more to herself than to anyone else. "It's close to being healed, but it still needs time."

Donnie winced as he lay back on the couch, feeling a familiar twinge of discomfort as the anesthetic began to fade. "We can't go to a doctor," he replied hoarsely. "It would get that EMT in trouble. He said he wasn't supposed to do that."

Jordon paused, looking up at him with a knowing look. "Who said anything about a doctor?" she teased gently, pulling out the bag the EMT had sent with them. Inside, she found everything she needed to finish what had been started. A syringe. More staples. Gauze.

Donnie's brows furrowed. "You ever do that before?" he asked, trying to hide the nervousness in his voice.

"No," Jordon answered, her voice surprisingly calm. "But I've watched it done enough. That EMT was right. Anyone doing this stuff except a doctor could get into all kinds of trouble." She filled the syringe with local anesthetic, the needle a sharp contrast against the soft, steady rhythm of her breathing.

An hour later, Donnie was resting, his breathing deep and steady as the pain finally eased. The local anesthetic had done its job, and his body, exhausted from the ordeal, finally gave in to sleep.

Jordon, cleaning up the mess, looked over at Vera, who had been silently watching from the doorway.

"Is this a better deal?" Vera asked, her voice a mixture of curiosity and concern.

"Much better," Jordon said with a small smile, her tired eyes glimmering with a quiet sense of pride. "He should be healed in time for the wedding."

Meanwhile, Raemundo had delivered his load of bear grass to the warehouse in Agua Prieta. The border guards, always friendly and smiling, made him feel welcome, but today, there was an edge to their politeness, a chill in the air he couldn't ignore. He tried to shake it off and focused on the task at hand.

As he stepped from his truck, the door of the warehouse rolled up, and two of his Indian workers came out, immediately starting to unload the truck. Raemundo barely had time to stretch his legs before he saw the fat tattooed thug step out from around the corner of the building.

"Hey, compa," the thug sneered, "you ratted us out to the border guards, didn't you?"

Raemundo froze, his gut tightening as he scanned the area. Two more men emerged from the shadows, their dark eyes cold, calculating.

"No, I didn't tell anyone anything. Why do you say that?" Raemundo's voice was even, though his pulse quickened.

"Immigration was waiting on my boys down the road," the fat man spat. "They got the load, and those boys are dead. I think you had something to do with it." His voice grew louder with each word, venom dripping from his every syllable. "I want my money back. Now."

Raemundo's hand twitched toward the gun at his side, but he held back. The two Indian workers behind him stepped forward, their hands gripping thick two-by-fours. Raemundo saw the faint glint of anger in their eyes, ready for action.

"I did what you asked. I delivered, and I didn't talk to no one," Raemundo said, trying to steady his breath. "The money's mine. I earned it."

The fat man took another step closer, his belly jiggling with each movement. "I want that pinche money, compa, or I'll cut your heart out!"

Raemundo stood tall, not backing down. His Indian workers moved closer, their presence strong and threatening. "I wonder how much lard your carcass could yield, compa," Raemundo said coldly, staring the man down. "Maybe we'll use your fat to grease the bear grass."

The fat man hesitated, his eyes flicking nervously to the men behind Raemundo. Before he could respond, the thwack of a two-by-four hitting his skull echoed through the air. He crumpled to the ground in an unconscious heap.

The workers moved quickly, loading the three bodies into the false floor of the truck. Raemundo climbed into the driver's seat, his face a mask of cold indifference as he drove toward the border.

At the port of entry, the border guards were still polite, their smiles as fake as ever. But Raemundo could sense their suspicion in the cold air as they waved him through. He was no stranger to their watchful eyes.

As night fell, Raemundo pulled over just outside Douglas. The chill of the night air bit at his skin as he lit a cigarette, the flame briefly lighting up his face. Above him, he heard a faint hum. He looked up, catching a glint of silver against the dying light of the sunset. A helicopter, distant but steady, followed his every move.

He leaned back in the seat, taking a slow drag from the cigarette. It wasn't until dark that he made his way to the back of the truck, dragging the bodies out into the dirt. He knew these men were on the wanted list, and by morning, the Border Patrol would find them. Dead bodies showing up along the border was nothing new.

Raemundo's truck hummed steadily as it rolled down the darkened road, the headlights casting long shadows on the barren landscape. He was oblivious to the fact that just a half mile behind, a Border Patrol truck was parked in the shadows, its engine turned off to avoid detection. The officers inside had been watching him for nearly an hour, their trained eyes scanning every move, every subtle shift in behavior. They had seen him come through the checkpoint earlier, polite as ever, his demeanor giving away nothing. But now, as they observed him drive past the last known crossing point, their suspicions were confirmed. The way he had slowed down just before reaching the city limits, the slight hesitation as if checking the rearview mirror—things didn't add up.

One of the officers, a seasoned agent with sharp eyes, leaned forward in his seat, his hand resting lightly on the radio. "That's him," he murmured. His partner, a young agent on assignment from another agency was still learning the ropes of surveillance. The young man nodded slowly, watching Raemundo's truck grow smaller in the distance. They didn't need to talk much; they knew the score. This wasn't the first time they'd seen someone like him—someone who knew how to fly under the radar, how to move with a calm, calculated confidence that made it difficult to pinpoint exactly what he was up to.

As the truck disappeared from view, the younger agent shifted uncomfortably, but his partner remained still, his eyes scanning the horizon. "We'll let him go for now," the older agent said, his voice steady and his words heavy with experience. The route Raemundo was taking was clear—heading back toward the ranch, straight into a maze of familiar dirt roads and quiet corners where eyes turned a blind eye to things that didn't quite meet the law. The agents knew what he was transporting. They knew he wasn't alone. The bodies, the cargo—it was all part of a bigger operation they had been tracking for weeks.

The older agent picked up the radio, his fingers moving with precision. "Hold off on the follow," he said, his voice low and controlled. "He'll be back. We'll catch him when it's time."

They were silent after that, watching the faint dust trail in the distance as Raemundo's truck continued its journey. The younger agent glanced at his partner, unsure of what came next. But the older officer merely sat back, his eyes narrowing as if seeing the entire unfolding situation in his mind. They weren't going to catch him tonight. But soon, they would.

The truck rumbled on, unaware of the watchful eyes that had been tracking it every mile.

Chapter 6

Two weeks before the wedding, Donnie had Jordon remove the stitches from his side. The wound looked mostly healed, but there was a dark, angry red welt where it had sealed over. He complained of itching, the skin taut and uncomfortable, and he desperately wanted to scratch at it. Jordon, standing beside him, grabbed his hand gently but firmly to stop him from doing so. With a quiet sigh, she smeared some soothing ointment on the scar, the cool cream offering instant relief.

The mornings were busy now, with the cows starting to calve. After tending to Donnie, Jordon would saddle up a horse and head out into the pasture to check on the cattle, making sure none were struggling with calving. The ranch had never felt more alive, the sounds of newborn calves bleating in the distance, the soft swish of hooves on dry ground. Donnie, too, kept busy, throwing himself into the daily tasks around the ranch. He patched fences, cleaned the barns, and even started rebuilding his father's roping arena, which had fallen into disrepair from disuse over the years.

Jordon had tracked down Mike, who was on the road in California, and though he assured them he would make it back in time for the wedding, his absence still weighed on her mind. Vera, ever the busybody, had Cliff two-stepping around, preparing everything for the event. Jordon and Vera spent their nights huddled together, going over the plans—food, decorations, and the endless little details that made up a wedding.

Jordon's parents had promised to be there the day before the event, so the pieces of the puzzle were finally falling into place.

Four days before the wedding, Jordon and Donnie saddled their horses for another round of cattle checks. She made it clear that Donnie wasn't to overexert himself, especially with his still-healing incision. Donnie smiled at her and nodded, but Jordon wasn't entirely convinced he'd follow her instructions. She knew him too well—stubborn, determined, and often reckless in his pursuit of a task.

Cliff watched them ride off from the barn, his gaze lingering on the pair as they disappeared into the distance. A small, content smile tugged at his lips. He thought to himself that life, from here on out, would only get better.

As they rode, Donnie couldn't resist the urge to play with his rope, throwing loops at bushes and rocks. The soreness in his side was minimal, and he reveled in the small victory of feeling like himself again. Jordon kept reminding him not to overdo it, but Donnie's smile was wide, his mind distracted by the simple joy of a well-thrown loop.

When they reached the area where the cattle were scattered, they split up to cover more ground. Jordon had planned to meet up with Vera later that afternoon to work on her wedding dress, so they worked efficiently, riding slowly through the brush and washes, checking on the cows and making sure none of them were having trouble calving.

Donnie rode over a low hill and dropped into the valley below, where the familiar sight of the Palmeros' camp greeted him. But something was off— the camp was a mess. Food and supplies were scattered across the ground. Tents were slashed and torn. The red bobtail truck sat abandoned on flat tires, the driver's side door hanging open.

The burros lay sprawled a few yards away, all of them shot in the head. Donnie's heart skipped a beat as he scanned the wreckage, the air around him thick with an unsettling stillness.

He dismounted and started to search the area, his mind racing. That's when he found the first of the workers. He was lying partially in a washout, his body crumpled awkwardly. His head was bashed in with a rock. Donnie's stomach churned as he forced himself to keep going.

Minutes later, he found the others, all six of the men who had been with the Palmeros, each one dead with crushed skulls. There was no sign of Raemundo. Donnie stood frozen for a moment, taking in the carnage. His breath quickened, and he felt a cold shiver run down his spine.

With a grim determination, Donnie turned his horse back toward Jordon. He spurred the horse into a lope, urgency driving him forward. As he crested the low rise, he spotted Jordon a quarter of a mile away, riding out of a low draw. Donnie waved his arms, yelling for her to turn back toward the house.

Jordon, startled at the sight of Donnie's frantic gestures, spun her horse around and spurred it into a lope to catch up. When she reached him, Donnie's words came tumbling out in a rush, the terror and disbelief in his voice impossible to hide. He told her what he had found—the camp, the bodies—and that they needed the law.

He clutched his side, grimacing at the twinge of pain, but he assured her he was fine. She wasn't convinced, but there was no time for arguing now.

When they reached the ranch, Cliff was waiting, his instincts sharp as ever. He could see something was wrong by the way they were riding in. Donnie jumped off his horse and explained the situation as quickly as he could while Jordon stripped the saddles from their horses.

Cliff didn't waste any time. He'd already started his pickup and pulled it up to the barn, the engine rumbling as Donnie jumped in. Without a word, they headed toward Douglas, the tires kicking up a cloud of dust behind them as they raced toward town.

Cliff and Donnie returned about an hour later, the dust from their tires still hanging thick in the air as they pulled back into the ranch yard. They weren't alone. Two Border Patrol units and a sheriff's deputy followed them, their trucks kicking up a cloud of dirt as they rolled to a stop near the campsite.

Cliff and Donnie stayed in the truck as the officers disembarked, stepping carefully around the wreckage. The Border Patrol agents and the deputy spread out, their eyes scanning the bodies, the wrecked camp, and the destruction scattered across the ground. One of the Border Patrol agents approached the truck cautiously, his boots crunching on the dirt as he moved around it, peering underneath and through the cab.

When he reached the back of the truck, he slid the gate open and began lifting up one of the false floorboards. A chill ran down Donnie's spine as the man called out to the others. "Hey, over here!"

The other agents and the deputy hurried over, their faces going grim as they saw what lay beneath the floorboards. Raemundo's body was slumped inside, his hands tied tightly with twisted barbed wire, the strands cutting deep into his flesh. A gaping hole in his chest, with dried blood smeared down the front of him, told a story of brutal violence. His mouth was frozen in a wide, silent scream, his expression forever frozen in agony.

Cliff stared in disbelief, his hand instinctively reaching for the side of the truck for support. "Who would do something like this?" he muttered, his voice thick with horror.

The lead Border Patrol officer, a seasoned veteran with a no-nonsense demeanor, looked at Cliff and answered. "More and more, we're finding things like this. Sometimes it's the cartels, sometimes it's other gangs. MS-13, the Aztecas… They don't come over here, but I think this was a revenge killing. We found three of their guys along the side of the road some time back. Their heads bashed in. The Aztecas… they're careful not to come across the border, but they're ruthless and bloodthirsty. Their stock and trade is weapons—unmarked guns, usually. We think Raemundo was hauling them across the line in this truck."

Donnie stepped forward, his voice tight with concern. "Are we in any danger from these Aztecas? Are they going to come after us?"

The officer considered the question for a moment before answering. "I don't see why they would. But they've got a twisted way of thinking. If I were you, I'd go armed when you're out here. They didn't drive in; they walked. Walked in, walked out. We're bringing in some dogs to make sure, but if they drove, you would've seen them."

The agent bent down and carefully replaced the boards over Raemundo's body, his eyes cold and professional despite the gruesome scene before him.

Two ambulances rolled up, their sirens muted now, parked behind the Border Patrol trucks. A service truck followed, pulling up to the bobtail truck to begin working on its tires. The ambulance attendants slipped body bags over the lifeless bodies of the workers, carefully securing them for transport.

The Border Patrol leader explained, "We can't do anything about the dead burros or all this other stuff here. We'll load it all into the truck. When the wrecker arrives, we'll haul it all back to your ranch. Then, we'll take it into town to the food bank and second-hand stores."

Cliff stood next to the ranch truck, leaning against the front fender, his gaze distant as he took it all in. Donnie approached him, watching as Cliff seemed to absorb the weight of everything that had just happened.

"Well, I got us in a hell of a mess this time," Cliff said quietly, shaking his head. "I should've listened to you when you said you had a bad feeling about that guy. Who knew it would end up like this?"

Donnie didn't answer right away. He knew the weight of guilt was heavy on Cliff's shoulders, but there was no changing the past. He placed a hand on Cliff's shoulder and said, "What's done is done. We can't go back. We've got a wedding to think about now. All we can do is keep our eyes open. But like the Border Patrol said, we didn't do anything wrong. Why would they come after us?"

Back at the ranch, Donnie and Cliff stood on the porch, watching as the caravan of ambulances, patrol trucks, and service vehicles passed by. The wrecker pulled into the yard, and Donnie directed the driver to where the bobtail truck needed to be parked.

Jordon came outside, her eyes scanning Donnie's face for any signs of what had happened. "Why does Cliff look so sick?" she asked, noticing the strained expression on his face.

Donnie sighed, his gaze following the vehicles as they continued past the house. "He blames himself for this. He thinks it's all going to come back to us somehow. Raemundo died a pretty horrible death. They cut his heart out. I think that hit Dad pretty hard."

Jordon's eyes softened with sympathy as she moved closer to Donnie. "But we've still got the wedding to do," she said, trying to lighten the mood. "Did you get that dress all nailed together?"

Donnie grinned at her, pulling her into a quick hug. "I did. It's looking beautiful. Now, let's get everything back on track. We've got a wedding to get ready for."

Chapter 7

The next morning, Mike Garrett rolled into the ranch yard, his truck looking like it had survived a warzone. The paint was chipped, the grille dented, and dust caked every inch of it. His trailer, however, was still intact and carried his two horses, Paywindow and Paycheck.

"Am I late?" Mike asked, his eyes scanning the ranch as Jordon rushed up to greet him.

Donnie, stepping down from the porch with a grin, shook his head. "No, you're a day early, but that's good." He chuckled. "Where you been, pard?"

Mike grinned back. "When I got Jordon's message, I was leaving Chowchilla. I've been as far north as Spokane, and I was headed back to Arizona. Was gonna make a couple of ropings, but I just drove straight through." He motioned toward the trailer. "Where can I put Paywindow and Paycheck?"

"Come on, I'll show you," Donnie said, leading the way toward the barn. "I emptied a corral yesterday just for you."

Jordon skipped along beside Donnie, her brow furrowed as she glanced back at him. "We got enough room for the horses my folks are bringing to the wedding?"

"We'll make room," Donnie replied, flashing a grin. "We get this little party over with, we gotta get back in shape. Leg the horses up, and me too. I've gotten a little soft laying around all this time." He shot her a teasing look. "Why do you think I've been working that arena? I've got some steers coming next week off the border. And there's a handful of calves out in the pasture we can wean early for practice. I've got it all figured out."

Jordon shot him a stern look. "Everything except your side being fully healed. You flank one calf and pull everything loose, and there'll be hell to pay. The doctor said six months. It's only been three."

Donnie met her gaze, his grin fading just slightly. "Yeah, well… that's why I've been staying on the ground for the most part." He waved off the concern. "But don't worry. I'll be fine."

By the time they reached the barn, Mike had unloaded his horses and led them into the empty corral Donnie had prepared. The horses, while not thin, looked pulled down, their muscles tight from long hours of travel and hard use.

"They need a little time off," Mike said, watching as the horses buried their heads in the hay-filled feed bunk. "Living in that trailer hasn't exactly been a good thing for them."

Donnie eyed the horses thoughtfully, then glanced back at Mike. "They'll recover. They're tough."

Cliff walked up, leaning on the fence, looking at the horses with a smirk. "Mike, looks like they traded legs with a killdeer and lost their asses."

Mike grinned back, brushing some dirt off his hat. "I've been winning just enough to keep diesel in the truck and feed 'em once a day… me every other day. You know, eating's a habit, and you can break it if you try hard enough."

"Well, around here, there won't be no habit-breaking," Cliff said, chuckling. "Let's go see if Vera's got a leftover biscuit for you." He started toward the house, the others following along, laughing.

Later that day, Mike came into the house, an armload of dirty clothes in tow. "Can I wash these somewhere?" he asked, setting the clothes down in the doorway.

Jordon, who was passing by, took the pile from him without a word. As she sorted through the clothes, she looked up. "Is this all your clothes?" she asked, raising an eyebrow.

Mike scratched his head, looking sheepish. "Guess I'll need a fresh set for the wedding. I'll go into Douglas tonight after supper and see what I can scare up."

Jordon shot him a skeptical look. "Oh, no, you don't. If you go to Douglas by yourself, all you'll scare up is trouble at some bar. We've got whiskey here, and I'll go with you tomorrow to the dry goods store to get you some fresh duds."

Donnie, who had been standing behind Mike, shot him a knowing look. "Why, Donnie, you're gonna make your folks think I'm an outlaw or something," Mike exclaimed.

Donnie, already walking away, called over his shoulder, "You are."

Morning broke the next day with a hearty breakfast. Afterward, Cliff, Donnie, and Mike stepped out onto the porch. Mike leaned back, rubbing his swollen belly with a satisfied grunt. "Cliff, that Vera is one hell of a cook. How come you don't weigh in at 300 plus?" he asked.

Cliff raised an eyebrow and grinned. "Mainly 'cause I don't eat half a dozen eggs, a half pound of bacon, and six pancakes. Good lord, boy, where do you put it?"

Mike chuckled sheepishly. "I guess I did make a bit of a pig of myself, but it's not every day I get that kind of cooking."

Donnie stepped off the porch, tossing Mike a look. "I'll go unhook my truck so we can go to town."

"Oh no," Donnie cut him off, "We're taking my truck. I know what you're up to, and there won't be no time for hanging out in a bar. New clothes, and right back here. Period. You're gonna stand next to me sober tomorrow." Donnie grabbed Mike by the arm, dragging him toward the truck.

Mike skidded along, whining. "Aw, c'mon, Donnie! I'm just gonna get a new shirt, not start a fight."

Cliff stood on the porch, grinning at the scene. As Mike and Donnie made their way across the yard, Mike's complaints echoed back to him.

Vera stepped out of the screen door, drying her hands on a dish towel, a chuckle escaping her as she watched Donnie drag Mike away. "I guess Donnie knows Mike too well. I bet he won't let him out of his sight until he says 'I do' tomorrow."

In town, Donnie dropped Mike off at the western wear store, then drove down the block to the bank to check his balance. He still needed to buy a wedding gift for Jordon. After a while, he parked outside the store, waiting for Mike. But when he walked in, Mike was nowhere to be found. Frowning, Donnie spun around and stepped back outside, scanning the street.

Across the way, he saw the *Sombrero*—a bar that opened early in the day. Donnie's heart sank. He crossed the street and peered through the door. In the back, there was Mike, leaning over a pool table, lining up a shot. Behind him stood a Mexican man, leaning on his cue stick, watching.

Donnie noticed the man's outfit—a turtleneck sweater. For this time of year, it seemed a little overdressed. He walked inside.

"Come on, Mike. We gotta go," Donnie said firmly.

"Not yet, pard," Mike replied with a grin. "I'm up 200, and if I win this one, it'll be 250. Get a beer and sit down. This won't take long."

Mike cracked the cue ball and sank another shot, then walked around the table to line up another. Donnie wasn't having it.

"We don't have time for a beer. There's stuff to do at home. Come on."

Donnie glanced at the Mexican man, who was now looking at Mike like sour beans. The man snarled, "He has my money. No one leaves until I get it back."

Mike, unfazed, sank the 8-ball and casually picked up the cash off the table next to his beer. "I'm done. Thanks for the game," he said, turning to follow Donnie out the door.

The Mexican man raised his cue, ready to strike, but Mike was quick. With a smooth, practiced motion, he jabbed the end of his cue backwards, catching the man in the belly. The man doubled over, gasping for air.

"Let's go, Donnie!" Mike hustled past Donnie, and they made their way out the door.

Behind them, the Mexican man was still struggling to catch his breath.

On the way back to the ranch, Mike explained with a laugh. "I didn't like standing out on the sidewalk, and a cold beer sounded good. Then the Mexican hit me up for a game of pool. The hustler got hustled."

Donnie clenched his jaw. "You better stay out of town for a while. I'm thinking that guy's bad news."

Mike shrugged and laughed. "As soon as the party's over tomorrow, I'll move on. You don't want me around during your honeymoon."

"You're not going anywhere," Donnie snapped. "Those skinnies of yours are skin and bone. They need rest. You're staying here until I get some practice in, then we'll hit the road. But headquarters is here. You need to settle down a bit. This 'party' attitude has kinda taken over your life."

Mike was quiet for a moment. "I'll behave, but let me have a little fun."

Donnie shot him a sidelong glance. "Your idea of fun and 'normal people's' idea of fun are a little far apart. Just bite your lip, curb your desires. You won't die."

Mike slouched in his seat, looking out the window. "I might," he muttered under his breath.

Donnie glanced over at him, his voice hard. "No, you won't."

The truck's tires kicked up a cloud of dust as the boys rolled back into the yard. Donnie squinted, his eyes catching the sight of a light blue Ford pickup truck, its matching trailer parked in front of the trailer house. It was an odd addition to the usual quiet scene.

Jordon stepped down the wooden porch steps with a quick pace, her boots crunching on the gravel. She hurried over to Donnie, her eyes sparkling with excitement.

"Mom, Dad, and Jan just got here," she said, her voice bright. "Your mom's cooking up a big supper tonight for us all to get acquainted."

Donnie barely had time to respond before Jordon's gaze flicked over to Mike. Her nose wrinkled at the faint smell of beer still hanging in the air. The sharp scent mixed with the dry desert dust, clinging to the back of her throat. "It's a little early for that, isn't it?"

Mike didn't miss a beat, his lips curving into a lazy grin. "Damn, you're not even married yet, and you're acting like a wife."

Jordon tilted her head slightly, her brow furrowing. "Well, just so you know"—she turned sharply to face Mike, her eyes narrowing—"my sister is only 17. So, hands off."

Mike gave a mock salute, still rubbing his toe absently in the dirt. "I already got the word. I'll behave myself. It'll be hard, but I'll do it."

Before Jordon could retort, a Border Patrol truck came into view, the engine grumbling as it rumbled across the yard. The dust settled slowly, coating everything in a fine layer of earth. The officer climbed out, his boots crunching the gravel as he walked over to the trio standing in the yard. Cliff was making his way from the barn, his silhouette outlined against the setting sun. Vera stepped out from the screen door and leaned against the porch railing, watching.

The officer tipped his hat as he approached them. "Good morning," he said, his voice steady, almost formal. "My superior says if you want to claim that Bontail truck, you can have it. Raemundo had no known kin in Mexico, and since the truck was abandoned here on your property, it's yours for the taking. If not, we'll auction it off."

He paused for a moment, letting the words settle in the air. The dry heat of the desert seemed to thicken around them. The agent continued, his gaze flicking between Cliff, Jordon, and Donnie.

"We also got word from an informant that Raemundo had taken a $5,000 payment for hauling guns across the line. But we found no guns, and there was no cash on him or any of the men working with him. The Aztecas want their money back. But no one seems to know where it went or what he did with it."

Donnie looked over at Cliff, uncertainty flickering in his eyes. "Do we want that truck?" he asked.

Cliff rubbed his chin thoughtfully, looking at the truck, then back to the agent. "What do we gotta do? I guess we could turn it into something useful?"

The agent nodded, taking a step back. "I've got some paperwork for you to fill out. It'll take about a month or so to get a clear title if you want to wait for it."

"Well, it's not hurting anything just sitting there," Cliff said, his tone casual. "And it's not in the way. Where's the paperwork?"

The agent handed him the stack of forms. Cliff signed without hesitation, the scratch of the pen loud in the otherwise quiet yard. The agent took the papers, gave a final nod, and turned toward his truck. As the officer drove away, the dust swirling behind him, he called over his shoulder. "Don't drive it out on the road until the title comes in the mail."

The three of them stood there for a moment, the weight of the situation settling in the still air. But none of them noticed Mike slipping off, moving with a quiet purpose. He wandered toward the truck, his boots sinking into the loose dirt with each step. He walked around to the driver's side, and with a careful glance toward the others, he eased the door open.

He stood there for what felt like a long time, staring into the cab. His fingers brushed the door frame, but he didn't touch anything inside. His gaze was intense, studying every inch, every detail.

The wind shifted, carrying with it the scent of creosote and sagebrush, but Mike remained still, his expression unreadable. After what seemed like an eternity, he closed the door with a soft click and turned back toward the group.

Donnie, still standing with Cliff and Jordon, looked up as Mike rejoined them. His eyes narrowed, trying to read Mike's face.

"Find anything interesting?" Donnie asked, his voice casual, but with a hint of suspicion.

Mike's lips curved into a smile, but it didn't reach his eyes. "No. But that don't mean there isn't something interesting in there... besides bean burritos."

A cooler evening stretched on later, the fading light casting long shadows across the yard as they all gathered around the dinner table. Jordon's parents and her sister seemed to settle in quickly, their laughter filling the air as if they had always been a part of the family.

Gene, her dad, was a stocky man with sun-darkened skin. He worked for the railroad and, on weekends, roped cattle with a precision that came from years of practice. His deep, hearty laugh rumbled like distant thunder when something amused him.

Jan, her sister, was a slight girl with red-gold hair that caught the light as she leaned forward, speaking with an eager smile. She was a rodeo queen in the making, attending high school rodeos with the same passion her father had for team roping. She was also set to attend New Mexico State University in the upcoming term.

Jordon's mom, a woman with auburn hair and a full, infectious laugh, looked every bit the picture of warmth. She made everyone feel at home the moment they entered the house, her presence as comforting as the food she'd prepared.

Cliff and Vera quickly made themselves at ease, falling into conversations about cattle and old friends, but Donnie watched Mike carefully, his senses on alert. Mike had joined in only when spoken to, answering questions without offering much beyond the bare minimum.

As the meal came to an end, Donnie felt the familiar tension that always seemed to hover around Mike. He waited for the storm to break. The silence between bites was heavy, the clink of silverware and the sound of Jordon's parents talking around the table seeming to fill every corner of the room.

When Mike finally stood, excusing himself, he didn't look at anyone. He just walked toward the room he shared with Donnie, his footsteps light but deliberate.

Donnie's gaze followed him for a moment before he turned back to the table, still sensing something off in the air. Whatever was coming, he knew it wouldn't be long before it revealed itself. And he wasn't sure they'd be ready for it.

Chapter 8

The day of the wedding went off without a hitch. It was held in the living room of Cliff and Vera's house, with only eight people in attendance, not counting the preacher. Vera had outdone herself with a grand luncheon, champagne all around, and an atmosphere filled with warmth. The house smelled of freshly baked bread, seasoned meats, and the earthy undertones of the desert outside. Donnie kept waiting for Mike to say or do something that would blow the lid off, but Mike was a complete gentleman—so much so that even Jordon's dad, Gene, seemed to take a liking to him. Jordon and Donnie sat in a state of disbelief, their minds spinning, yet nothing untoward happened.

After lunch, with just a single glass of champagne, Mike excused himself, saying he needed to check on his horses. He strolled down the path to the barn, the crunch of gravel beneath his boots loud in the otherwise peaceful afternoon. Once he was out of sight of the house, he ducked around the front of the International bobtail truck and moved to the driver's side door. He carefully opened it, ensuring no sound escaped, and once again peered inside the cab.

Being a bit shorter than the others who had been around the truck, Mike had the advantage of being able to look up under the dashboard while standing on the ground. There, high up and nearly invisible in the back of the dash, was a plastic-wrapped bundle, taped securely to some of the wiring. Mike had only spotted it by chance the first time he'd looked up into the cab days before.

With practiced ease, he pulled out his pocketknife and sliced the tape holding the package in place. As it fell to the floorboard with a soft thud, Mike's heart skipped a beat. He quickly tucked the knife away and scanned the area for anyone nearby. Seeing no one, he reached in slowly and picked up the round, plastic-wrapped package, his fingers trembling slightly.

When he peeled back the corner of the plastic, a crisp hundred-dollar bill was exposed. His pulse quickened, and a shiver ran through him. He hastily rewrapped the package, stuffed it into the front of his shirt, pulling the tail of his shirt outward just enough to conceal the bulge. Closing the truck door with the utmost care, he took a deep breath before heading toward the barn to tend to his horses, pretending nothing had happened.

He lingered there for a few minutes, letting time pass, before heading back toward the house, feeling a self-satisfied calm settle over him. In his room, he tucked the roll of cash into his shaving kit, zipping it shut with a quiet snap. He stood for a moment, savoring the feeling of having secured it, then returned to the party with the same composed expression as before.

By mid-afternoon, Jordon's family had left to return to Deming, and Donnie had moved his personal belongings into the mobile home that he and Jordon would now share. Cliff and Vera, with Mike's help, were cleaning up the remnants of the party. The scent of champagne lingered in the air, a faint reminder of the celebration.

Unbeknownst to them, half a mile east of the ranch, the Aztecas had set up an observer on a hillside with a telescope. On a 24-hour watch, the observer had seen Mike in the red bobtail truck. Though he couldn't tell exactly what Mike had done, he knew something had happened. His instincts told him it was important. The observer quickly packed up the telescope and tore off toward Agua Prieta, knowing he had to report what he'd seen.

Donnie was finishing his breakfast on the first day of being married. Jordon stood at the kitchen sink, preparing to wash the dishes. They had purposely slept in this morning, enjoying each other's company. Donnie took the last morsel of biscuit and swabbed up the loose egg yolk on his plate. He popped it into his mouth, savoring the warmth, and washed it down with the last swallow of coffee.

With a satisfied sigh, he carried his dirty dishes to the sink and slid them into the hot, soapy water. Wrapping his arm around Jordon's waist, he snuggled up to her and planted a sloppy kiss on her neck.

"Get away from here!" Jordon playfully pushed him away. "Don't you have something to do outside?"

Donnie grimaced and held his side. "That didn't hurt you much last night, bub. Get out there and earn a living," Jordon said with a sly smile.

Donnie walked to the door, took his hat off the rack, and shook his head. He opened the door and spotted Cliff and Mike walking toward the barn. He stopped, then returned to the house. Pulling open a drawer on an end table, he retrieved a snub-nosed .38 revolver.

"I almost forgot this," Donnie said, holding it up to Jordon.

"When can you quit carrying that thing? I don't like it," Jordon frowned.

Donnie just shook his head, tucking the gun into the waistband of his jeans as he turned to leave.

As he walked toward the barn, Donnie noticed something was off. He didn't see Cliff or Mike feeding the stock or moving about. The barn seemed eerily still. When he got closer, he heard angry voices. He slowed his pace, not wanting to stumble into an argument between Cliff and Mike. But as he approached the back end of the red bobtail truck, he realized it wasn't them talking.

Up near the front of the truck, on the driver's side, Donnie saw Mike and Cliff backed up against the vehicle, while three Azteca gang members stood in front of them, holding Uzi machine pistols. The pool player

Mike had worked over was standing in front of Mike, a serrated knife held under his nose.

"Look, gringo, where is the money?" the pool player sneered. "My man over there saw you take something out of this truck. I want my money before I cut your heart out! You remember what Raemundo looked like? That's gonna be you two in just a minute, and the other three up at the house will follow. Now, where's the money?"

Mike snarled at the pool player. "I don't have your money. I knocked the wind out of you once before, I'll do it again."

Donnie stood frozen for a moment, pride swelling in his chest at Mike's defiance. But the situation was escalating fast. Reaching into his back pocket, Donnie withdrew the .38, unsure if he could actually pull the trigger but knowing it might be the only way to save his friends, his dad, and his wife.

Clasping the revolver with both hands, he stepped around the end of the truck, pointing it at the pool player.

"Drop the guns and the knife! NOW!" Donnie shouted.

When the gang members turned their heads, Mike's right hand slid behind his back and reappeared with a 9mm pistol. In one fluid motion, Mike stepped up behind the pool player, wrapped his left arm around the man's neck, and pulled him in front of his body.

With lightning speed, Mike raised the pistol over the man's shoulder and fired three shots as fast as he could. The three Aztecas crumpled to the ground, neat holes just above their ears where the bullets had struck.

The pool player began to squirm, reaching back with the knife to try and stab Mike. But Mike, still holding the man in front of him, turned the gun downward and shot him in the knee. The Mexican screamed, dropped the knife, and fell to the ground, clutching his knee with both hands.

Mike leaned over him with a cold smile. "I told you I'd knock the wind out of you."

Cliff and Donnie stood dumbstruck, mouths agape, unable to process what had just happened.

Mike turned to Cliff. "You better go call the law. Tell them we need a meat wagon."

Reaching down inside his boot, Mike retrieved a black leather wallet and handed it to Donnie, who opened it to find a small badge and a letter stating that Mike Garrett was an agent for the Alcohol, Tobacco, and Firearms Department (ATF).

Donnie was speechless. "H-how long you been doing this?" he stammered.

Mike sighed. "When I dropped you off here after Santa Fe, they approached me about doing this. Before we met, I worked for a contractor who did nasty things to nasty people. ATF was finding all these guns up and down the West Coast. That's why I was rodeoing over there. Then, when Jordon called me to come here, it all just fit. And yes, I have the money this *pinchee* here is looking for. It's evidence."

"I really didn't want to get you all wrapped up in this, but now that you showed up, I'm glad. The boss told me to get a live one, and there he is. Unless I miss my guess, he's the jefe—the boss of the whole bunch. And when they're done with him, they'll know everything he knows, and he won't remember a thing."

"Dammit, you mean I've been traveling with an assassin this whole time?" Donnie sat down on the running board of the truck, shaking his head in disbelief. "All that crazy stuff you did was an act?"

Mike gave a half-smile. "No, it wasn't an act. That's me, alright. But it just worked into this real well. Don't worry, as soon as this is wrapped up, I'll take off. I don't want to jeopardize things with Jordon or your folks."

Jordon, who had been listening from behind the truck, stepped into view. "Mike Garrett, you're not going anywhere. We've got rodeos to make, calves to brand, and fences to mend here!"

Mike looked up at her and smiled. "I'd like that. I'll get the ATF outta here, then settle in... if just for a while."

Part II: Mike Garrett

Chapter 1

It wasn't quite sunrise when Mike stepped out the screen door onto the porch of Cliff and Vera's house. The morning air was crisp, laced with the faint scent of dew-soaked mesquite and dust that promised another dry day. The sharp, slightly bitter taste of black coffee still lingered on his lips, and a red-headed wooden match dangled from the corner of his mouth, an idle stand-in for a toothpick. He sank onto the porch steps, the worn wood creaking beneath his weight, and opened his box of Copenhagen snuff. The sharp, earthy aroma hit him as he packed a pinch into his lip, the familiar sting a small comfort. Yet, boredom had already taken root, gnawing at the edges of his thoughts.

Despite the bounty of life here, Mike couldn't shake a restless hollowness. Cliff and Vera treated him like family, offering warmth and acceptance he hadn't known in years. Every day, he roped in the boss arena with their son, Donnie, feeling the adrenaline rush of catching a clean loop. Donnie's wife, Jordon, always made sure his clothes were clean and ready, the scent of sun-dried cotton and soap clinging to his shirts. It should have been enough—but it wasn't.

Four months earlier, he had torn apart the Azteca Mexican Border gang, doing things that lingered in the dark recesses of his mind. Things he pushed away as he tried to fit into the gentler rhythm of ranch life. When the job was over and the adrenaline dissipated, he became the easygoing man everyone liked. Cliff and Donnie had offered to pay him cowboy wages for staying on, but he'd refused, preferring the quiet barter of room, board, and feed for his two horses. Still, the gnawing boredom persisted.

He'd helped brand calves, the acrid scent of singed hair and the high-pitched bawling ringing in his ears long after the work was done. Cliff roped and dragged them, Mike flanked and threw them with precision, while Jordon and Donnie branded, earmarked, and inoculated the young stock. The heat of the sun baked their sweat into a sticky film, and the sharp tang of blood and antiseptic clung to the air. But even in those moments, when the sweat stung his eyes and his muscles ached with effort, boredom hovered like an unwelcome shadow.

When Donnie had recovered from an injury and was fit enough to rope, they'd traveled to Benson for a few jackpot ropings. The nights were filled with the cheers of the crowd, the clinking of spurs, and the scent of leather and arena dust. They'd won a few times, pocketed some money, and celebrated with rounds of whiskey that burned on the way down. Yet, Mike always found himself tipping the bottle a little too much, numbing himself against the restlessness. The ride back home in the deep hours of night, with the desert wind cold against his face, only deepened the ache inside him.

The shootout at the ranch replayed in the back of his mind at odd moments—the echo of gunfire, the sharp metallic scent of blood, and the wild thud of his heart. He'd written a resignation letter, a simple two-page goodbye to that violent side of himself, but it ended up crumpled and forgotten in his file. The ATF had locked up Julio Martinez, the gang leader, in the federal prison in Eloy. Under the influence of chemicals, Julio had spilled every secret he had before his mind turned blank and broken, leaving him as nothing more than a hollow shell. It should have brought Mike peace, a sense of closure, but it hadn't. The fire inside him was too used to burning, and now it smoldered, unfed but present.

From his perch on the porch, Mike's eyes followed the shifting shapes of morning—the silhouettes of the barn and the corrals. He could see Cliff down at the barn, the older man's movements steady and reliable as he fed the horses. The faint whinny of a mare and the rustle of hay stirred something in Mike, a momentary flicker of peace. But the hollowness didn't let go.

He was a wizard with a heel rope, never missing a catch at a jackpot or rodeo. His hands knew the dance, the subtle shift and twist that spelled victory. He was a good traveling partner, a steady hand with horses, and the man who'd killed three and maimed another in cold efficiency was buried deep. Only Jordon, with her quiet glances and tension that never quite eased, reminded him that the wild man within still cast a shadow. Donnie's assurances had calmed her somewhat, but Mike could feel the wariness like a hidden splinter.

The morning light crept over the horizon, spreading a muted gold across the desert. The coolness of the night lingered for just a moment longer before the sun's promise of heat surged forward. Mike sighed, the sound heavy in the stillness. The world was waking, vibrant and alive, but inside him, the silence remained.

Chapter 2

Donnie drove through the expansive stretches of Arizona, the miles rolling under the truck's tires like a slow river. But as they neared the California state line, exhaustion claimed his heavy-lidded eyes. Mike glanced sideways, noticing the subtle droop of Donnie's head, the way he blinked longer than a heartbeat. In the trailer, Jordon lay curled up, unaware of the struggle up front.

"Pull over, Donnie," Mike ordered, his tone brooking no argument. Donnie opened his mouth, a protest forming on his lips, but Mike cut him off with a sharp look. "I said pull over; you're gonna get us in a wreck."

Reluctantly, Donnie veered to the shoulder, the tires crunching against the gravel and dirt as he brought the rig to a stop. The night sky stretched above them, deep and vast, absent of moon or stars. The only light came from their headlights, twin beams piercing the darkness. Mike swung out, the cool desert air brushing against his face, sharp with the scent of sagebrush and dry earth. Sliding behind the wheel, he waited for Donnie to shift into the passenger seat, then took the truck back onto the road. The silence was thick but comforting, and the rhythmic hum of the tires soon lulled Donnie into a deep sleep. Mike tightened his grip on the steering wheel and pressed down on the gas pedal.

"We'll be there by sunup," he muttered, eyes narrowing on the horizon where the dark seemed unending.

As the first slivers of dawn painted the sky in hues of burnt orange and gold, Mike guided the truck into the Bakersfield rodeo grounds. The scent of damp hay and manure met him as he stepped out, a familiar fragrance that spoke of early mornings and hard work. He rubbed his tired eyes, the weight of sleepless hours pressing on him. Donnie's snores still drifted from the open window. Mike chuckled and shook his head, the weariness tugging at his smile.

He moved with practiced efficiency, unloading their horses, their hooves thudding dully on the compact dirt as he led them to the portable stalls across the lot. The morning air was cool, tinged with the acrid bite of fresh alfalfa. He secured the last gate and turned just in time to see Jordon striding toward him, two water buckets swinging from her hands.

"Let me water them, Mike," she said, eyes bright despite the long drive. "Go get some sleep. The slack doesn't start until noon. I'll feed and water them."

Mike paused, feeling the exhaustion claw at him. He handed her the hose, watching as she immediately began filling the buckets. The horses dipped their noses in eagerly, the water sloshing over their muzzles. Mike bent down, pulled the hose to his mouth, and drank deeply.

The metallic tang of hose water filled his mouth, cool and refreshing.

"I'll sleep in the truck," he finally said, his voice rough. "You and Donnie use the trailer. Maybe stir up something to eat in a bit." He wiped his mouth and trudged back to the truck. Donnie was stirring, the spell of sleep loosening as he blinked awake. Mike grinned as he pointed toward Jordon.

"She's over there. Keep it down; I'm going to bed."

The rodeo grounds were alive with activity, the stock contractor's crew moving with purpose as they fed and prepped the livestock. The crisp snap of bales of hay splitting open, the lowing of cattle, and the stomp of restless hooves filled the air. One of the workers caught sight of Mike crawling into the truck cab and elbowed his partner.

"Aw hell, he's back," he whispered, shaking his head as he tossed another bale into the feed truck.

The sun was higher when Mike and Donnie saddled their horses in the warm-up arena. The scents of dust and sweat mixed with the sweet undertones of leather and saddle soap. The thrum of anticipation rippled through the rodeo grounds as the slack began, a low murmur of voices punctuated by the clang of metal gates and the occasional shout. Mike ran a hand down Paywindow's neck, the horse's muscles quivering with energy beneath his touch. The steady rhythm of his own heart matched the horse's pulse, a synchrony born of countless hours spent together.

When their number was called, Donnie led the way, eyes flicking to Caleb Driggers who leaned casually against the fence.

"Steer breaks hard left," Caleb advised. Donnie nodded, a flicker of gratitude in his expression before he turned his focus back to the task at hand. He positioned his horse in the box, reins taut, body coiled with anticipation. Mike shifted his weight, his heel loop ready, fingers brushing the coarse fibers of the rope, the scent of sun-warmed horseflesh sharp in his nostrils.

The gate flew open, and the world narrowed to the rush of hooves and the blur of motion—pure instinct, pure adrenaline.

Chapter 3

At the end of the Saturday performance and the first go-round, Mike and Donnie had secured the 5th spot in the top twelve. However, in the tie-down roping event, Mike struggled with a stubborn calf. The animal's muscles tensed as Mike flanked him once, but the calf twisted and bucked violently. Gritting his teeth, Mike flanked it again, the strain searing through his arms and shoulders. He managed to tie the legs swiftly, but the stumble had cost him dearly. One second—a single heartbeat—kept him from making the top 15 for Sunday. Disappointment gnawed at him, the thrill of competition momentarily soured.

Jordon's barrel run had been breathtaking to watch—her horse's hooves thundered against the packed dirt, leaving fleeting plumes of dust in their wake. Yet, in the end, she fell short by a mere two one-hundredths of a second. A sharp pang of frustration creased her brow, though her breakaway roping had lifted her spirits. Her 2.2-second run had drawn gasps from the crowd and placed her securely in second. A brief smile, rare and fierce, had flashed across her face when the announcer called her time.

The night had settled around the rodeo grounds, a velvety shroud punctuated by the low hum of conversations and the distant whinnying of horses. Mike sat in a folding chair outside the trailer, a glass of bourbon in his hand. The sharp, oaky flavor burned pleasantly as it slid down his throat, warming him from the inside. The air was thick with the scents of sweat, horse tack, and the faint tang of hay carried by the gentle breeze. He gazed out into the dark horizon, watching the stars flicker like embers caught in the vast, obsidian sky. This—the road, the rodeos, the pulse of anticipation before each run—this was what he had longed for. Yet, the quiet moments on the ranch, serene and predictable, felt suffocating in comparison.

He glanced over his shoulder at the trailer. The warm, golden light spilling from the window outlined Donnie and Jordon in a tableau of laughter and whispered intimacy. Their smiles and easy touches reminded Mike that he was an outsider here, a third wheel rolling in the shadow of their world. A dull ache settled in his chest as he took another sip, the loneliness biting deeper than any saddle sore.

A sudden shift in the air drew Mike's attention, and he turned to see Cyrus Reynolds—an old friend and fellow rogue—sauntering out of the shadows. Cyrus's grin was a familiar blend of mischief and camaraderie. "Cyrus! Where ya been?" Mike's voice lifted, the weight in his chest momentarily lightened.

"I've been around," Cyrus replied, eyes twinkling with the kind of trouble they both relished. He pointed to the bottle in Mike's hand. "Got any more of that tonsil varnish?"

Mike smirked, reached under his chair, and pulled out a second bottle. "Have at 'er, pard."

Cyrus took a deep swig, the liquid swirling up the neck of the bottle as he drank. When he lowered it, a gleam of satisfaction danced in his eyes. "I'm headed downtown to the Crystal Palace," he said, wiping his mouth with the back of his hand. "Yokum's playing tonight, and that's where the rodeo dance is. You wanna go?"

Mike looked back at the trailer, its light now muted as if the world inside was slipping into a quiet dream. The hollow feeling nudged at him, demanding he fill it. "Yeah, let's go." He pushed himself up and followed Cyrus, humming a carefree tune and throwing a playful shuffle step into his stride. The promise of chaos glinted in the air.

Hours later, the dance hall pulsed with life. The Crystal Palace was a cacophony of stomping boots, laughter, and fiddles twining in a feverish melody. The scent of spilled beer and smoke mingled with the sweet notes of cheap perfume. Mike spun a petite, dark-haired girl in circles, her laughter ringing clear as bells. The rush of the night surged through him, and for once, the ache dulled.

Cyrus, ever the charmer, had drawn his partner into a shadowed corner. His voice, smooth as honey, murmured promises only heard once a year when cowboys were in town. But the spell snapped when a man in a battered hat and scuffed boots stumbled toward them, fists clenched. "She's my fiancée!" he shouted, fury bright in his eyes.

Mike turned just in time to see Cyrus square up, his fists coiled tight. The ensuing scuffle was swift and brutal, Cyrus's right hook finding its mark and sending the man sprawling. Gasps swept the room as the girl darted away, eyes wide with alarm.

The dark-haired beauty Mike was with pulled loose and followed her, saying, "She's my friend."

Out of the door came a couple of burly bouncers with a bad look about them. Cyrus turned to meet them, but Mike saw discretion as the better part of valor. He grabbed Cyrus by the arm and dragged him out the side door. The booze was gone, the girls were gone, and Mike had to rope the next day. The party was over.

Chapter 4

Someone was tugging on Mike's foot. He grumbled and shifted to one side, but the tugging continued. With a reluctant squint, he opened one eye and saw Donnie standing over him, holding a steaming cup of coffee. Sunlight streamed through the truck's windshield, heating up the cab and making Mike break into a sweat.

"You better get up, Mike. You got company," Donnie said, nodding toward the two policemen standing in front of the trailer. Mike let out a miserable groan, slid off the truck seat, and shakily stood, taking the cup from Donnie with a grateful nod.

"Are you Mike Garrett?" one of the officers asked, his eyes fixed and serious.

"You know I am. What can I do for you?" Mike took a long sip of the coffee, trying to steady himself. Behind the officers, Donnie struggled to contain his laughter, hand clamped over his mouth. Jordon stood in the trailer doorway, eyes blazing with tension.

One of the policemen pulled a small, dog-eared notebook from his pocket and flipped it open. "We have a few questions regarding last night's altercation at the Crystal Palace."

Mike groaned inwardly. "Do you know a Cyrus Reynolds? And a young lady named Alma Jenkins?"

"I know Cy. Can't say I place the girl, though. Why?" Mike's eyes flicked up over the rim of the coffee cup, searching for answers.

"We have a warrant out for Mr. Reynolds on assault charges," the cop explained. "Miss Jenkins claims you were present when the incident occurred."

Mike's brows knit in confusion. "I didn't know her name if she's the one I was dancing with. And Cyrus only hit the guy twice. Then the girl I was with took off after the girl Cyrus was dancing with. Why?" he added, trying to make sense of it all.

"Were you aware that Miss Jenkins is only sixteen years old?"

Mike's hand froze mid-sip, and the coffee cup slipped from his fingers, crashing to the ground. His eyes went wide, disbelief washing over his features. "Hell no! She was in the club; I assumed she was of legal age. How in the hell did she get in there?"

"Her father secured a pass from the owners," the cop said, his tone hardening. "Her father is the justice of the peace."

Behind the officers, Donnie's muffled laughter finally burst out, while Jordon's glare could have cut steel.

"Miss Jenkins claims you made improper advances toward her just before Mr. Reynolds assaulted the victim, who, incidentally, is the son of the chief of police. He lost two teeth and sustained a broken jaw," the cop continued, leaning forward. "Now, where is Mr. Reynolds?"

"Look," Mike said, voice cracking as he tried to regain his composure, "when Cy dropped me off last night, he mentioned heading back to Tucson. And I swear, if I'd had any clue that girl was underage—I didn't know. I don't even know why Cy hit the guy. I just pulled him out of there after it happened. I had no idea it got so bad." His words stumbled out in a rush, tinged with guilt and exhaustion.

The officer's eyes narrowed. "Well, if you see him, let him know we're looking for him. And for your sake, I'd advise you to get out of town as soon as the rodeo wraps up."

Without another word, the policemen turned and walked back to their cruiser. Donnie finally let out a laugh that doubled him over, while Jordon's glare stayed pinned on Mike, a storm brewing in her dark eyes.

Chapter 5

Mike gripped the wheel, the sun sinking low behind him as he guided the rig eastward. The sky was streaked with the warm hues of dusk, painting the landscape in soft golds and deep purples. He reached up to tilt the rearview mirror away, cutting the glare from his eyes. The cab of the truck felt hollow, filled only with the static rhythm of a Chris LeDoux tape playing low. Donnie and Jordan were tucked away in the living quarters trailer, leaving Mike alone with his thoughts as the miles unraveled beneath him.

They had just left the rodeo grounds, and as the rig rolled past the entrance, Mike noticed the two local cops parked by the gate. He offered a casual wave, but their eyes tracked him with hard, unfriendly stares. He let out a slow breath, shaking off the tension. Despite the dicey situation with Cy, the weekend hadn't been a total loss. They'd done well—Donnie and Mike had claimed victory in the short go and snagged second place in the team roping average. Jordan had triumphed in the breakaway roping, earning herself a shiny buckle and a smile that wouldn't quit. Between them, they'd made out with nearly three thousand dollars in prize money.

Mike smirked at the memory of Donnie laughing so hard Sunday morning that he'd split open his scar, blood trickling down his cheek as he doubled over. The laughter had been a welcome sound, a reprieve from the weight that had settled on Mike's chest. At 34, life seemed to be one long string of questions without answers. His friends were finding roots, carving out families and homes, while he still chased a thrill that always led him somewhere half-lit and lonely.

Jailbait situations weren't his idea of a good time—that much had been hammered home by Cy's reckless stunt. Mike's jaw tightened at the memory. Four years of skirting trouble had frayed his nerves, and he was done gambling with the kind of odds that might see him shelved for good. But stepping away from the ranch, from the people who'd taken him in, felt wrong. He'd been living on borrowed kindness. Still, he needed a plan, something more than just aimless rides and dusty motels.

He wasn't ready to hang up his spurs. Not yet. But maybe a quieter existence, one with fewer close calls and fewer cops at the gate, wouldn't be so bad. With his bank account sitting healthy, the idea of finding a secluded patch of land and laying low carried a certain appeal. The thought lingered as he glanced down at the fuel gauge, the needle dangerously flirting with 'E.' A stop was non-negotiable.

Crossing the Colorado River, the neon glow of a truck stop came into view. It looked worn and tired, the kind of place where stories ended and others began. The lights over the fuel pumps flickered, a warning he couldn't ignore. As he pulled off the highway, four

Harley Davidsons loomed near the front door, chrome glistening under the harsh fluorescent lights. Two riders sat astride their bikes, eyes shaded by mirrored sunglasses. The uneasy prickle that climbed Mike's spine made him shift in his seat. But the rig was gasping, running on fumes.

He reached for his 9mm, tucking it into the waistband of his jeans before stepping out. The nozzle clicked into place as he started to pump the fuel, eyes darting between the riders and the road.

"Hey," a voice came from his right, thin and urgent. A woman approached, her steps hurried.

Mike's eyes swept over her. She was young, with dark hair pulled into a messy ponytail and a wary look in her eyes. "You with them?" he asked, nodding subtly toward the bikers.

"Not by choice," she whispered, her voice shaking. "I'm scared."

Mike's jaw tightened. "Get in," he said, tilting his head toward the passenger side. "Stay low and keep me talking. Got it?"

The woman darted around the truck and climbed in, her eyes wide and panicked. Mike's gaze didn't waver as he watched the two bikers by the door. Suddenly, the glass front of the truck stop burst open, and two more men stormed out, eyes searching wildly.

"Lorna!" one of them shouted.

Mike's pulse quickened, but he kept his movements slow and deliberate as he replaced the fuel nozzle. The bikers exchanged glances, cursing as they mounted their rides and roared out of the lot, tires spitting gravel.

Back in the cab, Mike put the rig in gear and eased back onto the highway. The silence inside was thick, broken only by the dull thrum of the engine.

"Thank you," the woman said after a moment.

Mike glanced at her briefly, then back at the road. The flash of red and blue lights lit up the side view mirror as two police cruisers barreled past them in the opposite direction. Mike's fingers brushed the handle of his 9mm, and he holstered it with a sigh. The woman watched, eyes wide.

"Would you have used that?" she asked, voice barely a whisper.

"If I had to," Mike replied, his tone matter-of-fact.

They drove on, the road stretching into the dark, unanswered questions trailing like shadows behind them.

Chapter 6

Mike gripped the steering wheel, barreling through the night with the truck aimed eastward, cruise control set at 80. The young woman in the passenger seat, Lorna, had sat up and observed him. Her blonde hair framed her face, blue eyes sparkling against her tanned complexion. She smiled, revealing brilliant white teeth. Mike realized she was closer to his age than he initially thought, offering a sigh of relief reflecting on the troubling encounter in Bakersfield.

Curious, Mike asked, "What were you doing with that trash back there? You don't fit in with their crowd." His eyes stayed on the road.

"I was hitchhiking. They stopped to pick me up, and when I said no, they just grabbed me and took me along. I've hitched all over the U.S. and never had a problem until now. That might be my last time," she replied.

"Well, it ought to be. An attractive girl like you, you could get in a lot of trouble. What made you think I would be any better than those guys?" Mike glanced at her from the corner of his eye.

"You're a cowboy. Cowboys are gentlemen, mostly. I'm an army brat. My mother died when I was 12, and my dad put me in the best boarding schools he could afford. When I turned 17, I started hitching in the summer just for the fun of it. Cowboys always treated me right," she explained. "My name is Lorna. What's yours?"

"Mike, Mike Garrett. How far do you need to go? I'm going right through Phoenix and Tucson."

"Do you know where Cochise is? I teach school there. We've got a long weekend, so I was going to hit the beach. But I gave that idea the slip when I got picked up by the bikers. I just want to go home."

"Well, Lorna, Cochise is right on my way. We're headed home to Douglas. My partner and his wife are sleeping in the trailer back there. It's their folks' outfit. So, I'll just take you all the way home, and in exchange, you can keep me company and not let me go to sleep. Fair enough?" Mike sneaked another peek at her bright smile and long legs. "I've never had a schoolteacher look like that," he thought to himself.

Lorna sat up straight and relaxed. They talked through the night. She shared stories about the school, teaching 2nd grade. Eventually, she asked about the pistol: "Do you always carry that gun?"

"Mostly, but I won't use it unless forced to. It used to be part of my job. But I want to move on from that. I'm just going to rodeo and maybe settle down someplace."

"What was your job?" Lorna inquired.

"The company had a slogan. I did nasty things to nasty people. I can't say anything else right now. But I wasn't a very good person. I've done a lot of things I'm not too proud of. I just want to move on," he confessed, glancing at Lorna, who bowed her head, her face turning white.

"You've got nothing to worry about. You're not a nasty person, are you?" Mike grinned at her. "I hope not. I do kind of like you. It's hard to imagine you as a bad guy."

She looked up. "Well, quit hitching around the country for kicks, and I'll keep you out of trouble," Mike suggested, laughing.

As the sun began to rise over the Chiricahua Mountains, they reached Lorna's house. She grabbed her bag, slipped out, and circled around to Mike's door. Giving him a big kiss, she said, "Will I see you again?"

"You can bet on it, Blondie. I'll be back Saturday if that's good?"

"Saturday morning, and I'll have breakfast ready when you get here." She bounced up the steps and waved as she entered the house.

Mike pulled the rig back onto 191, heading south to Douglas. Still an hour from the ranch, he didn't notice time flying by, and the thought of being bored had disappeared.

Chapter 7

The sun rose with full force as Mike steered Donnie's rig into the ranch yard. Cliff, meeting them at the barn, noticed Mike alone and questioned why he hadn't let Donnie relieve him. Mike, grinning, explained that he stopped to let his copilot out, referring to Lorna, who had kept him awake and engaged in conversation all night. Jordon, blushing, unloaded the trailer with Donnie.

Cliff, chuckling, put his arm around Mike's shoulder. "Vera has breakfast on the table. Let those two put the horses away, and you tell me about the weekend." Cliff and Mike headed towards the house.

The next five days passed in a whirl of activity. While Donnie and Jordon rode every day and checked the cows, Mike stayed busy cleaning and maintaining his truck and trailer, working on various ranch equipment. Cliff marveled at Mike's diverse skills and remarked to Vera about his capabilities. Despite his talents, Cliff couldn't fathom Mike's seemingly carefree and reckless attitude. Donnie had mentioned that Mike made a lot of enemies during their year of traveling, but he also had never had a more loyal friend.

Friday morning, Mike unhooked his truck from the trailer and parked it at the house without explaining his plans to anyone. Cliff, curious, speculated that Mike might have found a girl somewhere. Vera dismissed his conjectures, telling him to mind his own business. Mike spent Friday doing domestic chores, not wanting to be a burden on Vera.

At 5 A.M. on Saturday, before anyone except Cliff was up, Mike drove out of the yard without saying a word to anyone. Cliff wondered if Mike had found a girl.

Mike took the Cochise exit off 191 and idled through the small residential neighborhood. As he turned the corner to Lorna's house, he saw a motorcycle parked in front. Anger surged through him, but he parked across the street, and as he stepped out, his hand instinctively found the handle of his pistol. Shielded by the open door, he slid the holster behind his belt in the small of his back without realizing it. Stepping up on the porch, he found Lorna at the screen door, her hand signaling distress.

Lorna opened the door, her hand signaling distress. "Look who's here," she stammered. "Come on in; I have breakfast ready for you." Mike nodded and entered the house. At the table sat a skin headed, tattooed, muscular man, Darren, with a cup of coffee and a sour expression — the same man from the truck-stop a week ago.

"She ain't got enough breakfast for both of us, so I guess you better go on. Besides, I don't think we need any shit kickers around today," Darren said.

Mike looked at Lorna, her face pale. "Is that what you want, Lorna?" he asked.

"No, I want Darren to leave. He wasn't invited. He just showed up a little while ago," her voice trembling.

Mike turned back to Darren. "Okay, bub, you just heard the lady. Drag your freight and don't come back."

Darren approached Mike menacingly, but when he was close, he suddenly weakened. Mike had the pistol out and pressed it into Darren's lips, ordering him to open his mouth. Finding Darren's mouth dry, Mike instructed him to back up. With the pistol pressed against Darren's mouth, Mike forced him out the door, blood trickling from the corner of Darren's mouth.

Mike then checked Darren's bike for weapons and flung a Bowie knife across the street. He ordered Darren to leave and never come back, warning that if he did, it would be open season on him. Darren nodded, and Mike sent him flying down 191 towards Interstate-10.

Turning to Lorna, Mike asked casually, "Is breakfast ready?" She was leaning against the door jam, pale and scared. "You do nasty things to nasty people, don't you?" she said.

"Only when they call me a shit kicker," Mike replied, stuffing the 9mm in the holster. "All this week, I've thought of nothing but this breakfast with you. And then to find that skinhead here, I guess I just lost my cool."

"Lost your cool? I never saw anyone so cool in my life. I think you would have shot him and never batted an eye," Lorna said, still in shock.

Mike pulled out a chair and sat down. "I almost left the gun at home. The last thing I wanted was to have to use it again. I want to put all that behind me. There was a time when doing something bothered me for days, but I think I became calloused to it. I don't know if I will ever move away from that, but when it comes to someone I care about, it won't take much to get me started, I guess. It's just a reaction, I guess."

Lorna set a fresh cup of coffee in front of Mike with a plate full of fried eggs, bacon, and a fresh biscuit on the side. "I know that's not much, but I haven't had time to go to the store this week."

"Where do you go?" Mike asked between mouthfuls.

"Benson, to the Walmart there. Okay, we can go in a bit; I'll push your cart. I want to see what domestication feels like," Mike grinned, and Lorna laughed. "I'm glad you came back," she said.

Chapter 8

For three consecutive weekends, Mike showed up at Lorna's house on Saturday morning for breakfast, and each day they spent together became special for him. As they grew more comfortable with each other, Mike's ease and warmth became more evident. The ranch crew, witnessing this transformation, couldn't believe how different Mike had become. He was no longer suspicious of everything around him and embraced the chores and repairs around the ranch. Donnie and Cliff were astonished at the positive change in his attitude. Vera, however, warned them that the old Mike might not be too far beneath the surface.

Despite the positive changes, Lorna couldn't shake the memory of Mike with the pistol jammed in Darren's mouth. Mike reassured her that she had nothing to fear from him, but the image lingered in her mind.

As the weekend of the Lordsburg Rodeo and County Fair approached, Lorna agreed to join Mike. They planned to take his rig, while Donnie and Jordon would bring his rig to meet them at the rodeo. Late Friday evening, the Road Forks Truck Stop came into view. Mike pulled in and suggested they have supper before continuing. In the back of the truck stop's parking lot, a bonfire blazed, accompanied by loud music. A Hidalgo County deputy sitting in his car watched as Mike parked next to him and asked about the celebration. The deputy explained that it was a biker group out for the weekend and assured Mike that his rig would be safe parked next to him while they ate inside.

Entering the cafe, they witnessed two burly bikers holding a third between them at the cash register. The middle biker, squirming, eventually produced some cash, and the cashier counted out what was due before pushing the rest back to him. The two bikers warned him not to try skipping out again, and as they turned to leave, they spotted Mike and Lorna. The one who spoke earlier noticed Darren, the biker in the middle, running out the door. Mike shrugged and joked, "Guess cowboys scare him."

After supper, they returned to the rig, finding the deputy gone and two bikers sitting on the hood of Mike's truck. Instinctively, Mike reached into the small of his back for his pistol before realizing he had left it in the truck. Seeing this, Lorna felt a little scared. Mike whispered to her, "Just walk right on by and get in the truck like there's nothing wrong." As they approached, the bikers slid down and reassured them that everything was still there, waving as they walked back toward the bonfire.

Lorna flashed a dazzling smile at Mike in the dark of the cab. Mike started the truck and eased out of the parking lot onto I-10, heading towards Lordsburg. Unbeknownst to them, a motorbike with a skin headed rider pulled out of the shadow of the cafe building, following at a safe distance.

Chapter 9

When Mike and Lorna pulled into the Lordsburg fairgrounds, the main parking area was empty, illuminated by a bright moon and a light breeze. All the corrals at the arena were full, so they tied their horses to the trailer for the night and retired to the front of the trailer in the small living quarters.

The next morning, Mike woke up to the sound of horses pawing the trailer. As he got dressed, he realized Lorna wasn't there. Stepping out, he saw her coming up the driveway from town with bags in hand. She went for breakfast, bringing pastries, breakfast burritos, and coffee. While Mike took care of the horses, she made coffee, and they enjoyed a pleasant morning.

As Mike carried water buckets to the hydrant, something heavy struck the back of his head when he opened the trailer door. The lights went out for a moment, and when he came to, he found himself lying in the parking lot. Arms unresponsive, he heard footsteps running away. A warm, wet sensation dripped down his face. Trying to rise, he realized his arms didn't work.

Lorna, Donnie, and Jordon rushed to him. They sat him on the trailer steps, and Lorna brought hot water and a clean cloth. Jordon, a nurse, started washing the blood from the side of Mike's face. Donnie, concerned, asked, "Who did this, Mike?"

"I don't know, I didn't see him. Just heard him running away. What the hell hit me?"

"A steel pin from your trailer divider. It's got blood on it. You got a good-size gash. It's gonna need a couple of stitches. We better get you to the hospital."

"No hospital, just patch me up here. Can you do it, Jordon?"

Jordon hesitated, expressing concern about a possible fractured skull. Mike reassured her, saying he left his gun inside that morning, and he never saw the attacker. Lorna sighed in relief. Jordon cleaned the wound and suggested an x-ray, but Mike insisted on being treated there.

While they waited, a security cop from the fairgrounds arrived, stating he saw the incident and called the local law. The cop took their statements, and a city cop arrived to continue the process. As they discussed a possible ambulance, Mike grew impatient and short-tempered. Eventually, the security cop and city cop left.

Jordon, now assisted by Lorna, sewed up the wound with three stitches. Mike endured it without a sound until the alcohol swab touched the wound, prompting a loud holler.

"Don't be a hero; take these ibuprofens and lay down. We'll take care of everything," Jordon advised.

Mike forced a smile, assuring them he'd be fine for the rodeo. As Donnie reminded him of the one-header format, Mike grinned and said, "Just come get me 30 minutes before I rope. I'll be okay."

Jordon, with a hint of admiration, remarked to Donnie, "I knew he was tough, but I don't think he felt a stitch. I think he only hollered about the swab so I would think he was alive."

"Well, that's Mike for you — no quit," Donnie replied, pondering if Mike was putting on a show for Lorna.

"If he was, I think he made his point," Jordon said, her expression serious.

Chapter 10

Someone tugged at Mike's foot, persistently pulling him from the grip of sleep. Lorna stood at the foot of the bed, a sweet smile on her face, announcing it was time for the rodeo, cowboy. Despite the pain shooting through his head, Mike carefully slid off the bed, rising slowly. Jordon, standing behind Lorna, voiced concern, asking if he wanted to turn out.

"Yeah, I'm sure. Give me a minute for this drum to stop pounding in my head," Mike replied. Leaning on the trailer for support, with Lorna balancing him on the other side, he made his way to Paycheck, his horse, who stood ready with a calf rope on the saddle horn. Lorna held him by one arm, and with a head bowed forward, he mounted the horse, still wobbly on his feet.

Lorna continued to support him as he went to the warm-up area, loping Paycheck to warm him up. Mike looked like he could fall off at any moment, yet somehow, he remained on the horse. Donnie, watching from the fence, observed that Mike appeared pale but swung the rope as if nothing was wrong. When called to rope, he rode into the box with his loop in hand. Though he looked dazed, Mike swung the rope skillfully, and when he nodded for the calf, Paycheck left with a jarring start. The rope cinched up around the calf's neck, and despite the bone-jarring stop, Mike managed to flank and tie the calf.

When he signaled time, he just sat there, dazed. The field judge urged him to get back on his horse to finish the event. Mike, seemingly in a fog, walked back to Paycheck. As he settled into the saddle, Donnie was there, steadying the horse. Donnie grinned up at him, "You're one-tenth out of the money, pard, but no one with a sore head would have done it better."

In the team roping slack, Mike achieved the seemingly impossible by heeling Donnie's steer by two feet, throwing under his horse's neck and catching the steer on the left side. "Damn pard, if that holds up, we win second," Donnie exclaimed as they rode back to the trailer.

At the trailer, Mike slid off his horse into Lorna's waiting arms, saying, "I think I need a nap." Three days later, he woke up in his bed at the ranch with Vera watching over him. Though his head still throbbed, the pain had lessened, and the world stopped spinning when he sat up. Vera, fussing over him, mentioned that Lorna had gone home but promised to be back Friday night.

"Doc says you gotta stay here at least another day. So just settle back. You hungry? I'll go get you something," Vera offered, expressing her concern. Mike inquired about Lorna, and Vera explained that she went home not to miss work but would return Friday night. Vera smiled and remarked, "I like that girl. I think she's good medicine for you."

Mike nodded, saying, "Yep, she has my number alright. But for some reason, I just can't seem to stay out of trouble. You think this will ever end?"

"I think so, things run in cycles, so maybe this one is winding down. At least you haven't had to shoot anyone," Vera remarked with a smile.

"Yet," Mike added, touching the stitches on the side of his head.

Chapter 11

Friday evening, the drone of Mike's truck filled the air as Lorna rolled into the ranch yard. Excitement twinkled in Mike's eyes as he sat on the porch of Vera and Cliff's ranch house. Lorna, with her long tousled blond hair, hopped out of the truck, flashing a brilliant smile. She leaned down, giving Mike a long, slow kiss, her hand running down his back as she casually tucked his holster into the back of his pants.

"I brought your friend for a visit," she cooed in his ear.

"Did you think I was lonesome for him?" Mike teased. Lorna winked at him, pulling a chair close to his.

"You never know when you need a friend, huh?" she remarked. Mike held her hand, smiling at her, "I kinda hoped I could discontinue that friendship."

"Later. How's the head? Your color is better. Do you still get dizzy and headaches?" Lorna inquired.

"A little, not as bad as before. Vera has kept me on the straight and narrow, and Jordon comes twice a day to check on me. I'm covered up with attention, no matter how well-meaning it is," Mike said, smiling again.

"Remember the sign we saw at Cochise about a ranch for sale? Do you think you could stand a little road trip to check it out?" Lorna's eyes sparkled when Mike sat up in his chair.

"When? I'm ready now. Let's go!" Mike tried to get up.

"In the morning will be soon enough. I called on it yesterday. It runs 200 head, no house, just a couple of wells and corrals. I got a map in my purse. I'll show it to you later. It's held by an estate. The owner died two years ago with no will, been in probate all this time. The heirs don't want it. Does it sound like it's what you're looking for?" Lorna explained.

"Yes, it does. Did they price it?" Mike asked.

"No, they said go look at it, and then we talk. But it's going to be a lot for a rodeo bum, I bet," Lorna replied, ducking her head.

"Well, this rodeo bum might just fool ya," Mike laughed.

The next morning, full of anticipation, Lorna and Mike drove out of the yard at daybreak. Mike, unable to sleep all night, couldn't stop thinking about the possibilities of the little ranch. He knew 200 cows wouldn't make a living for him, let alone for him and Lorna together. But it would be a start, and he wasn't ready to quit rodeoing. He wasn't sure about Lorna's plans for teaching, but he knew they could make something work. Unless this little ranch was a plumb disaster, he was ready.

When Lorna pulled up to the gate, she reached into her purse, producing the map and a key on a ring. "When I got the map, they gave me a key to the gate," she explained. After pulling through the gate, she shut it and got back in the truck. Just as she clicked the lock shut, a motorcycle roared by. She walked back to the truck without looking at the biker.

"Was that that skinhead?" Mike asked.

"I don't know; I didn't even look up to see," she replied as they drove into the ranch. A windmill and a set of corrals with cattle scales came into view. The weeds grew knee-deep in the corrals, and the water storage tank overflowed as the windmill had been turned off. Mike got out to inspect the corrals and water troughs.

"Nothing's been here but deer and javelina. They told the truth about the cattle being removed," he said as he got back into the truck, pointing down the road. "Let's see the rest of this outfit."

By 2 o'clock that afternoon, they had explored every accessible corner of the ranch in the truck. The grama grass was tall, headed out, and no cattle tracks were in sight. The other windmill was pumping water, just like the first one. They pulled over under the shade of a big mesquite tree. Lorna had packed a lunch in a box that Vera had prepared for them. As they munched on sandwiches, Mike gazed across the land dotted with mesquite and a hint of prickly pear cactus.

Chapter 12

It was late when Lorna guided the truck back onto Houghton Road in Tucson, the city lights flickering in the distance like scattered embers. The hum of the engine filled the silence, and Mike sat in the passenger seat, staring out the window as the darkened scenery swept past. The night air seeped through the cracked window, carrying with it the faint scent of desert sage and the coolness of a late autumn breeze.

"Do you really have that kind of cash lying around?" Lorna asked, keeping her eyes on the road, her hands firm on the wheel.

Mike's gaze remained fixed on the horizon, a distant expression clouding his blue eyes. "That and more," he admitted, his voice low and tinged with regret. "It's not just lying around, though. But by Monday afternoon, I'll have enough to cover the check for the ranch." He paused, drawing in a deep breath. "Doing the things I did in the past paid real well. I didn't spend much of it because, deep down, I knew it was tainted. I did some terrible things for that money, thinking I was doing them for God and country."

The truck's headlights illuminated the road ahead, casting long shadows over the cracked asphalt. The rhythmic thumping of tires on the uneven surface was the only sound for a moment before Mike continued, "When

I woke up to the reality of it all, I didn't know what to do with the money. So, I just let it sit there. You see, I don't ever want to kill or hurt anyone again. It's a bad feeling. You lie awake at night, wishing for daylight so you can try to forget the things you did. As time passes, you get calloused, but it never leaves you. It's always there, gnawing at the back of your mind."

Lorna glanced at him, catching the flicker of pain in his eyes. "Being with you has made it a bit easier to bear," he said softly. "I look at Donnie and Jordan and see what a good life they have. I hope we can find that, somehow." His eyes drifted back to the window, reflecting the pale glow of distant streetlights. "Those folks we met tonight were sure nice. The world needs more people like them."

Lorna's laugh was light, a hint of warmth against the cool interior of the truck. "They didn't know what to think when you wrote out that check," she said, amusement dancing in her tone. "And when you told them to call on the funds, no strings attached, just a handwritten receipt—I bet they thought you were crazy."

Mike's lips curled into a small smile. "I couldn't let that deal slip away. Besides, they can't draw on it until Monday. Writing it out was a calculated risk. But if I'm right, they'll hold off until we meet at the title company." He turned, his expression serious as he studied Lorna's profile, illuminated by the soft glow of the dashboard lights. "Is this a road you want to go down? Staying with me, knowing what I've been?"

Lorna's grip tightened slightly on the wheel, her gaze forward but thoughtful. "I've never committed to anything or anyone as much as I have with you. Don't ask me why, it just all fell into place. My only worry now is Darren. He's been around, but I think he's kept his distance because your truck has been parked at my house. Still… I'm scared," she admitted, her voice barely above a whisper. "That's why I brought you your gun."

Mike's eyes softened, a shadow of understanding passing over his face. "I thought so," he murmured. "I just don't want to use it again. Until I met you, my soul felt sick. I just hope he backs off, sooner rather than later."

The night pressed against the truck, an endless sea of darkness broken only by the faint glow of distant porch lights and the occasional passing car. Mike leaned closer to Lorna, his voice low. "You know, you—"

"Mike, I've got to drive," Lorna said, a hint of teasing in her voice as she pushed him back upright. "Besides, there's a motorcycle behind us."

Mike's expression shifted, the hint of tension returning. "I know. I've been watching him for a while. As long as he stays where he is, we're fine. Don't change anything. Just drive like you normally would." He exhaled, eyes narrowing as he peered into the side mirror.

"It might not even be Darren. There are plenty of motorcycles out there."

Lorna kept her eyes forward, the road stretching endlessly into the night. The hum of the engine and the steady thrum of their hearts were the only sounds as they pressed on, uncertain of what awaited them at the end of their journey.

Chapter 13

When Lorna and Mike arrived at the ranch, the house was shrouded in darkness, with only the distant chirp of crickets and the occasional hoot of an owl breaking the silence. Lorna tiptoed into the bedroom, the wooden floor creaking under her light steps, and collapsed into bed. Sleep claimed her within minutes, leaving the faint scent of desert sage clinging to her skin.

Mike moved quietly into Vera's kitchen, the familiar scent of old coffee grounds and spices filling the air. He reached for a glass and spotted Cliff's nearly empty bottle of Jim Beam on the counter. Pouring a generous amount, he made a mental note to pick up a new bottle when he next went into town. The bourbon burned as it slid down his throat, warming him from the inside. Glass in hand, he walked out onto the porch and sank into the wicker chair that Cliff favored. The cool night air wrapped around him, and he gazed out over the moonlit ranch, where the silver light painted long, pale shadows across the ground.

Mike imagined himself sitting on the porch of his own ranch one day, sipping his own whiskey, the land stretching out before him like a promise. The thought brought a rare moment of contentment. As the first hint of dawn brushed the eastern horizon with a faint pink glow, Mike heard the stirrings of life inside the house. He remained motionless, deep in thought, staring at the now-empty glass in his hand.

The screen door creaked open, and Cliff stepped out with a steaming mug of coffee. He paused, eyeing Mike. "Brought you a cup of coffee, but looks like you got a head start on the rest of us. You okay?"

Mike managed a thin smile and nodded. "Yeah, just thinkin' is all. What can I do to help this morning?"

Cliff's eyes softened with understanding. "Just sit tight until Vera gets breakfast ready. I'm going to feed the ponies." He took a sip from his mug and ambled down the steps, the scent of hay and dust swirling around him as he headed to the barn.

Mike watched him go, his stride easy and unbothered. "Not a worry in the world," Mike thought, a pang of envy tightening in his chest. He set the empty glass on the small side table and pushed himself up, heading for the corrals where Cliff had disappeared. He needed advice—guidance—and he knew Cliff was the one to ask.

Just as Mike reached the haystack, a shadow shifted, and Darren emerged from behind it. The man's eyes glinted with malice, and a smirk spread across his face, baring yellowed teeth. His shaved head shone in the early light, veins pulsing at his temple.

"I've been waiting for you, shit-kicker," Darren sneered. "We've got unfinished business."

Mike took a slow, steadying breath, every muscle tensed. "Look, Darren, I don't want any trouble. Just get on your bike and go. We'll leave it at that." He turned slightly, keeping one eye on Darren, trying to defuse the situation.

But Darren's response was swift. His hand lashed out, striking Mike hard across the face and sending him sprawling to his knees. The metallic taste of blood filled Mike's mouth, and the world spun as he struggled to regain his footing.

"I'll teach you to shove a gun in my mouth," Darren growled, stepping forward to deliver another blow. "And you're not taking my woman from me."

Mike's back slammed against the rough bales of hay, the scent of dried alfalfa and sweat mingling as he gasped for breath. He tried to push himself up, but Darren's shadow loomed over him, a fist raised.

"NO! Leave him alone!" Lorna's voice rang out, sharp and desperate. She rushed at Darren, grabbing his arm with both hands. Her eyes, wide with fear and fury, met his.

Darren snarled and shook her off, sending her stumbling backward. Before he could turn his attention back to Mike, Cliff appeared around the corner, eyes blazing. "Mike!" he shouted and, without hesitation, hurled a three-tine pitchfork in a swift, practiced arc.

Mike caught it mid-handle, the cool wood biting into his palm. In one fluid motion, he swung it toward Darren's outstretched arm. The center tine pierced flesh just above the wrist, while the outer tines sank deep into the haystack, pinning Darren's arm.

Darren let out a scream, the sound slicing through the morning air. His eyes darted between the blood seeping down his arm and the fury on Mike's face. He knew then—this fight was over.

Chapter 14

Three months later, Mike Garrett sat back in a hand-carved wooden chair on the wide front porch of his newly built ranch house, the golden light of sunset casting a warm glow over the rolling expanse of his land. The whiskey in his glass caught the last rays, glowing amber as he swirled it slowly and sipped, savoring the smoky burn. The scent of fresh-cut pine from the new construction mingled with the crisp, dry aroma of the Arizona desert evening.

The house had been completed just a week prior, and he and Lorna were still settling in, finding their rhythm in this newfound peace. He chuckled as he thought back to the day he, Donnie, and Cliff had gone to the sheriff's office to close the chapter on Darren's assault.

"I have good news and bad news, fellas," the deputy had said, leaning back in his creaking chair as the three men stepped into his cramped office. The room smelled of old coffee and dust, papers stacked haphazardly on every surface.

"The bad news is," the deputy continued, "the county attorney was going to set a low bail for Darren. He'd be back on the—"

Cliff's temper flared instantly. "What the hell do you mean?" he shouted, his voice like a whip crack in the room. "He trespassed on my ranch, assaulted my family, and he was going to—"

"Hold it, Mr. Boss," the deputy interjected, raising a calming hand. "Let me finish. The good news is that the FBI picked Darren up about an hour ago." The deputy's eyes gleamed with satisfaction. "Turns out he had federal charges waiting for him. Kidnapping, violating the Mann Act, unlawful detainment—no bail for those." The tension in the room broke like a snapped rope as a grin spread across the deputy's face. "Darren's on his way to Texas now, where he'll be tried for kidnapping a minor and bringing her across state lines. He's toast."

Mike remembered the way they had exchanged relieved looks, a heavy weight lifting off their shoulders. From that day, everything had fallen into place as if fate had chosen to smile on them.

Now, he hadn't carried a pistol in weeks. The specter of violence that had loomed over him for so long was finally fading. Even the letter from the ATF accepting his resignation had brought an unexpected calm. He took another sip of whiskey as the horizon deepened to violet, the chill of the coming night creeping into the air.

A cloud of dust rose on the dirt road leading to the house, and soon Donnie and Jordon's truck rolled to a stop. They jumped out, their boots kicking up more dust as they approached, arms full of bags and a bouquet of red roses. The scent of fried chicken wafted from the bags, mingling with the sharp tang of the desert.

Lorna stepped onto the porch, her smile warm as the day. Donnie climbed the steps and handed her the bouquet. "For the new home. A lady needs flowers to start off right," he said, his grin wide.

Jordon laughed as she handed Mike a gallon of Jim Beam. "And we brought this to christen the house," she said.

Mike cracked the cap with a practiced hand and raised the bottle. "Looks like we're starting off with fried chicken, whiskey, and good friends," he said, his voice deep with contentment.

Inside, Lorna and Jordon laid out the feast on the large oak table, its surface still smelling faintly of varnish. Lorna turned to Jordon, eyes shining. "I think Mike's finally figured out how to use all that money for something good. He's going to build an arena and give free classes to underprivileged kids who want to learn to rope. He's already reached out to an orphanage in Tucson."

Jordon's eyebrows shot up. "Is he going to quit rodeos?" she asked, a touch of disbelief in her voice.

Lorna's smile softened. "Oh no, he's planning to run at the circuit championships with Donnie. He has so many plans, I don't know how he keeps them straight. It's like he's a new person. When he goes to sleep at night—"

Just then, Mike walked in, the soft glow of the lamps catching the happiness in his eyes. "When I go to sleep at night," he said, finishing Lorna's thought, "I finally rest easy. And that's thanks to you."

Lorna's heart swelled as he wrapped his arm around her. They stood in their new home, surrounded by laughter, the scent of fried chicken, and the promise of all the tomorrows they could now share.